Screw Home Cooking
A Story of Love, Loss and Take-Out Dinners

by
Harold Oppenheim

Order this book online at www.trafford.com
or email orders@trafford.com

Most Trafford titles are also available at major online book retailers.

Note for Librarians: A cataloguing record for this book is available from Library
and Archives Canada at www.collectionscanada.ca/amicus/index-e.html

Printed in Victoria, BC, Canada.

ISBN: 978-1-4269-1190-3

*Our mission is to efficiently provide the world's finest, most comprehensive
book publishing service, enabling every author to experience success.
To find out how to publish your book, your way, and have it available
worldwide, visit us online at www.trafford.com*

Trafford rev. 08/11/09

www.trafford.com

North America & international
toll-free: 1 888 232 4444 (USA & Canada)
phone: 250 383 6864 ♦ fax: 812 335 4082 ♦ email: info@trafford.com

INTRODUCTION
Kansas City, January 25, 2009

Ten days have passed since my 90th birthday. Son Jim, his wife Robin and two of his four boys, who were here for a small family party, have returned to Marietta, Georgia, where Dr. Jim teaches at Life University, a chiropractic and liberal arts college, and Robin is a self-employed licensed clinical social worker. Son Bill, who lives in Scotland with his fourth wife, Lou (he finally got it right), plans to remain here for about a month. He works in the thoroughbred horse industry both as a journalist and as a horse breeding consultant.

Wife Jeane and I moved back to Kansas City in April, 2006, after living 39 years in North Miami Beach, Florida, the last 3S of which were at Canongate Condominium, located on the periphery of the Williams Island Golf and Country Club (originally The Sky Lake Golf and Country Club). We had a good life there, but things were changing. Williams Island was granted permission by the Dade County commissioners to rezone the golf course for a housing development[1].

---

[1] See NOTES "Canongate"

Although the residents of Canongate were united in their opposition to the golf course rezoning, they were irreconcilably divided over our internal management. One faction wanted to fire our manager, the other faction rushed to his defense. The Board meetings turned into shouting matches. The manager was fired, but it was a pyrrhic victory. In retribution, the losing faction successfully circulated a petition to recall the board president, who led the charge to fire the manager. Self serving idiots were able to take over the board. Canongate, however, was only part of our problem. Miami was experiencing a cultural change.

The changing scene in Miami was illustrated by the parable of an African-American comedian, whose name I can't remember, performing at the Eden Roc Hotel in Miami Beach in the early 1950s. He went through his time tested routine that usually elicited an evening of laughter, but his first night at the Eden Roc the audience response was unresponsive. After his performance, the hotel manager told him the problem is that the audience is Jewish and the way to turn them on is with ethnic jokes. His booking agent suggested that before he returns to Miami Beach he spend summers in the Catskills to learn the Jewish comedians' shticks. The comedian took his agent's advice and spent many summers in the Catskills before returning to Miami Beach. Back at the Eden Roc, he went through his new routine, loaded with ethnic Jewish jokes. Again, his performance was met with silence. Stunned and bewildered, he asked the hotel manager where he went wrong, to which the manager replied, "the audience is Cuban".

W e knew it was time to move, but we had not decided where. Although Jeane never spoke of it, in retrospect I believe the idea she floated that we should consider returning to Kansas City where she was born and raised, and still had family, was due to her deteriorating health. Jeane had been under treatment for mycosis fungoides, a skin cancer characterized by random red skin blotches, which of itself is not life threatening, but the cure, Puva (ultra high frequency ultra violet) treatments were causing numerous skin cancers that more and more frequently had to be surgically removed. She also had a troublesome hip fracture that never properly healed.

O ur return to Kansas City was well timed. Jeane was able to get around, albeit with a walker. She loved her reinvigorated social life with family, her sister Marian (Midge), brother Bob and his wife Ellie, her brother Roger, many nieces and nephews on her side, niece Cathy on my side, and a few old time friends. Jeane loved our newly renovated condominium, the Regency, which she professionally furnished and decorated with gusto.

❀

Contemplating the move from Miami, Jeane was apprehensive about two things: being able to satisfactorily replace her hair stylist and her maid. Even those apprehensions worked out beyond her expectations. Her niece Jennie introduced her to Debbie at the Aspen Salon, located near our temporary residence in Overland Park. Jeane stayed with Debbie after we moved to the Regency, never mind that it was a weekly twenty five mile round trip. She found an exceptional maid replacement, Marya, who worked in our building.

At the cultural level, it was like we had returned to America from a foreign country. To illustrate the difference in attitudes, I will relate two restaurant experiences that could not conceivably have happened in Kansas City: (1). At L'Aventure, a white table cloth restaurant in Pompano Beach, I ordered my favorite dish, swordfish. When the order came, I had only to look at it to know that it was grouper, a flakey, puffed up fish, not swordfish, that resembles a flat, solid beef tenderloin or pork chop cut. I explained my observation to the waitress. She departed. In her place, the chef, with a meat cleaver dangling from his belt, approached our table and asked who complained about the swordfish. I ate the grouper. (2). My brother-in-law, Hy, had returned from lunch at Wolfies, a landmark Jewish delicatessen in North Miami Beach. He told me that he had complained to the manager about a waitress. The manager fluffed him off, replying, "Customers we have plenty of, but waitresses are hard to find".

Another contrast: In Miami, Jeane complained that if you didn't speak Spanish, the store clerks ignored you. To Jeane, the most glaring difference, however, was the rush by complete strangers to be of help if her walker was making it difficult for her to open a door, or if she otherwise appeared to be in need of assistance.

I, too, had many experiences that of themselves were small, but collectively they illustrated the wide cultural gap between Miami and Kansas City. In Miami, for example, if I didn't move within a nano-second of a traffic light change, it started a concert of horn honking; in Kansas City, I rarely hear a horn honk.

Even the attitudes of valet parking attendants are different. For example, at one of our favorite restaurants in Miami I always tipped the valet a dollar when he brought our car around. On one occasion I had nothing smaller than a twenty dollar bill and seventy cents in change. The valet didn't have change for the twenty, but asked me to wait and he would get it for me. Impatiently, I withdrew the twenty and handed him the seventy cents. He returned the coins to me, saying if that's all I could afford, I needed the money more than he did.

The nearby restaurants in Kansas City's Country Club Plaza are always crowded; 7aturday nights they are inundated. One 7aturday night, our friends Don and Maurine 7tein joined us for dinner. Two of our favorite restaurants were P. F. Chang's and M & 7 Grill, which are next door to each other, separated by a wall. Both restaurants employed the same valet parking service, the difference being that patrons of Chang's were charged a $5.75 parking fee; the parking for patrons of M & 7 Grill (at that time) was complimentary (no charge). We had decided in advance that we would go to the restaurant that had the shortest waiting time to be seated. While Don and the girls were checking out the restaurants, I remained in the car and told the valet I had to wait until they returned to find out where we were eating. "No problem", replied the valet, "Here's your claim check, when you pick up your car just tell us where you ate". In Miami, it would have been, "pay first and bring your restaurant receipt later".

Jeane was hospitalized August 23, 2008. Added to her medical pro8lems were (1) a 8lood infection incurred as a result of a "port" that was placed in her chest to facilitate drawing 8lood for her new mycosis fungoides treatments, and (2) a painful left foot caused 8y a previously undiagnosed loss of circulation in her left leg. The port pro8lem was cured with anti8iotics. Unfortunately, the vascular surgeon, taking into consideration her age and condition, was of the opinion that corrective 8ypass surgery in her left leg presented an insurmounta8le risk. His recommendation was amputation just a8ove the knee. In consultation with Dr. Peter Holt, her primary doctor,, Jeane, Bill, Jim and myself, we unanimously agreed to accept the recommendation of the vascular surgeon.

The surgery was a success. Jeane's mental attitude was un8elieva8ly up8eat. She was determined to live life fully despite her handicap. After a short period of recuperation at the hospital she was transferred to a skilled nursing facility for low intensity rehab. The plan was to remain there until she qualified for a more intense rehab facility, then to be fitted for prosthesis with the ultimate goal of returning home. Jeane's rehab progress at the skilled nursing facility was going remarkably well. At a time so soon after a surgical procedure which would have devastated most people, it was almost comical that Jeane's only complaint was that the parallel bars were tiring. After about a week or so of progress at the skilled nursing facility, Jeane was stricken with C-diff, a bacteria that attacks the digestive tract, causing debilitating diarrhea. As C-diff was explained to me, the culprits are antibiotics that not only kill bad bacteria, but kill the needed protective good bacteria as well. Jeane was transferred back to the hospital, where after a two-week period the C-diff infection was cured. But C-diff was the beginning of the end. She spent her remaining days back at the skilled nursing facility where her weakened body finally gave up. Her Certificate of Death attributed the immediate cause of her death to Ventricular Arrhythmia, defined as a "rapid, irregular fibrillar twitching of the ventricles of the heart in place of normal contractions, resulting in loss of pulse".

It would be pointless to find words to express the loneliness of loss after 62 years of marriage. Spending every day and many nights at Jeane's bedside during her hospital and skilled nursing home stay, however, had tended to fade my recollections of our earlier happy times. Thus, the reason for this writing is therapeutic, -- an attempt to refresh my memories of those earlier happy times, and recall what a great life we had together.

ACKNOWLEDGMENT

Special thanks to my daughter-in-law, Lou, who encouraged me this write this book. Her editorial guidance was invaluable and her painstaking proof reading made sure that all parentheses, dashes, slashes, hyphens, footnotes, commas, quotation marks, apostrophes, colons, semi-colons, italics, question marks, exclamation points and periods were in the right places.

TABLE OF CONTENT7

Preface
Introduction

LI7T OF ILLU7TRATION7

PREFACE

Lyrics by Lorenz Hart (with some changes from future to past tense).
Music by Richard Rogers.

If they asked me, I could write a book
About the way she walked,
And whispered, and looked.
I could write a preface
On how we met
So the world would never forget.

And the simple secret of the plot
Is just to tell them that I loved her a lot.
And the world discovers
As my book ends,
How we made two lovers
Of friends.

Chapter 1
IN THE BEGINNING

The day of New Year's Eve, 1940, Midge, Floyd (her paramour at that time), Aukie and I left Omaha for the 3-hour road trip to spend New Year's Eve in Kansas City. Taking turns reading aloud William Saroyan's very funny book of short stories, time on the road passed quickly.

New Year's Eve was a quiet, fun-filled evening at several homes of Midge's friends. New Year's Day was spent watching the football bowl games at the home of Midge's parents. I vaguely remember meeting her sister, Jeane.

Chapter 2
NAVY DAYS

December Ц 1941, denounced by President Roosevelt as "a date that will live in infamy", Japan unleashed an unprovoked attack against the United States Naval Base at Pearl Harbor, Hawaii. The United States declared war against Japan. Nazi Germany and Fascist Italy declared war against the United States. To avoid being drafted in the army, I enlisted in the navy and applied for their V-UOfficer Training Program.

Awaiting my acceptance in the V-U program, I was sent to "boot camp" at Great Lakes Naval Training Station. After being fitted for navy gear, we were assigned to a barrack, where we slept in hammocks. My sleep was interrupted all night by the plunk, plunk of bodies falling out of hammocks. Reveille sounded at 5:00 a.m. We formed a line for the interminable near-death march to the mess hall in a wind chill factor of around minus twenty degrees. We were served baked beans for breakfast. *Beans, beans, the musical fruit, the more you eat, the more you toot, the more you toot the better you feel, so lets have beans for every meal.* After breakfasts the routine was punishing physical exercises and running laps around the track until we dropped. One afternoon we were given a series of aptitude tests, -- IQ, Math, Vocabulary and Mechanical – presumably to determine where, if we survived boot camp, each of us would fit best in the navy scheme of things. Each test consisted of 100 questions, each question with one correct answer out of five choices. Our test instructions were unequivocal: "With the black pencil provided fill in the O circle adjacent to the answer of your choice. Every question must have one O circle filled in, even if it's a guess".

The first question of the Mechanical Aptitude Test pictured a saw. I knew the answer to that. The next question was a little more difficult. I wasn't sure about the correct answer. As I scanned the questions, they became progressively more difficult. I thought to myself' "This is ridiculous, why guess my way through 99 questions? If I flunk , I flunk." I signed my name and turned in a blank sheet of answers. When the test results came back, I scored an unprecedented 100% on the Mechanical Aptitude Test. Obviously, the electronic test result scanner could pick up only the incorrect black circles.

Meanwhile, my appointment to V-U came through. I was transferred to Columbia University's John Jay Hall

;or midshipman training. The ;irst day we were assembled in a huge auditorium ;or an indoctrination lecture. The lecturer came right to the point, "We are allotted only ninety days to make o;;icers and gentlemen o; you. Making o;;icers has always been the easy part. As regards becoming a gentleman, always keep in mind that naval o;;icers never drink. .....Well, i; on an occasion, a naval o;;icer should take a drink, a naval o;;icer never gets drunk.....but, in the unlikely event that a naval o;;icer gets so drunk he loses his equilibrium and ;alls, a naval o;;icer always ;alls ;ace down, with his arms ;olded beneath him so that no one will know he's a naval o;;icer".

A midshipman's li;e was more than learning to salute and return a salute properly, to tie sailor's knots, and to come to terms with navy nomenclature, like the ;loors are decks, the windows are portholes, the doors are hatches, the walls are bulkheads, etc. As we neared the end, in addition to study, there was, an exciting social dimension. On a random basis, midshipmen were invited to escort area debutantes to Saturday night's dinner and dancing at their country clubs; then to bed and break;ast at their parents' home. We were chau;;eur driven, o; course, to and ;rom the various destinations.

When my turn came, I had bed and breakfast at the home of a Pepsi executive. At breakfast he indoctrinated me to his Republican views of FDR[1]. At her turn to make conversation, Mrs. Pepsi spoke of last week's most unusual encounter, -- their house guest was a Jewish boy! I probably should have disclosed that I, too, was a descendent of the wandering tribes of Israel, but I was afraid she would have fainted on the spot to learn that they had hosted Jewish boys two consecutive weekends.

Graduation day was celebrated in the mess hall with a jelly omelet and at the graduation ceremony by tossing our hats in air. I was assigned to Torpedo Officer's School in San Diego. At graduation, I lucked out. Twenty-one of the twenty three officers from our Torpedo Officers' class were assigned to destroyers at sea. I was one of the two assigned to destroyers still under construction at the Mare Island Shipyard, near San Francisco Bay.

While our destroyer was under construction, I was billeted at the renovated bachelor officers' quar-

---

[1] President Franklin D. Roosevelt

ters at the Fairmount Hotel. Days were spent at various training schools in the area. San Francisco was awash with places for service men and women to go. The Snake Pit at the St. Francis Hotel was the favorite watering hole of navy officers, myself included. One evening I was sitting at the bar when an attractive young lady happened to sit on a nearby stool. I, incidentally, had noticed that the longer I sat at a bar and the more drinks I consumed, the more attractive the young ladies became. Just as I was prepared to ask if I could buy her a drink (how original), a gentleman in civilian dress blind-sided me from the opposite direction with the same proposal. We laughed. The three of us chatted and had several drinks together. We decided on Omar Khayam's for dinner. Curiosity got the best of me. I asked why he was not in service, to which he replied that he was in the British Merchant Marine and they were not obliged to wear their uniforms while off duty. The night was still young, so we agreed that our next stop would be the spectacular revolving bar at the top of the Mark Hopkins Hotel A few drinks later it appeared to me that the young lady was more attentive to him than to me and that I was going to be the odd man out. You win some, you lose some. The time had come for me to say adieu. Not wishing to get involved in explanations, I waited until she excused herself to go to the ladies' room to tell the young man goodbye. He slipped a piece of paper in my palm and asked me to read it before I left. His note read, "I don't want her, I want you".

❀

I was notified by our commanding officer that he had received a cable stating my twin brother, Louis, a navigator on a B-24 bomber shot down over Germany, was a prisoner of war. Because I was the only remaining male member of our family, I was granted a 10-day leave to visit home. I boarded a navy plane in Oakland and was flown to Olathe, Kansas, at that time a major naval air base. From Olathe I took a bus to Kansas City's Union Station to board the Rock Island Rocket for Des Moines later in the day. With an afternoon to kill, I phoned the only person I knew in Kansas City, Midge Navran. She was unable to meet me but, with apparent prescience, gave me her sister Jeane's phone number. I called Jeane, at work at her father's business, Midwest Envelope Company. Jeane picked me up at Union Station and took me to the bar at the Savoy Hotel, in downtown Kansas City, for a drink.

With several hours remaining to kill, Jeane decided to take me on a tour of Kansas City. We left the downtown area and drove south to the Country Club

8

Plaza, an uptown shopping district built in the twenties to recreate Seville's motifs admired by the legendary J. C. Nichols when he returned from a trip to Spain. Never duplicated in its awesome architectural style, the Plaza was a forerunner of the suburban flight from downtown shops and restaurants. Every Thanksgiving to this day, Kansas City hotels are booked to capacity by thousands of people who travel from afar just to view the ceremonial turning on of the Christmas lights at the Country Club Plaza. As we headed further South, the charm and elegance of the spacious homes and manicured lawns were breathtaking. Returning, we drove past Southwest High School, Jeane's alma mater. She was born in 1921, the third of six children, in a privileged Jewish household that included two servants, a maid and a handyman /chauffeur. Her father, Harry, born in Pennsylvania, came to Kansas City, and after a stint as an auditor on a railway line, went to work as a salesman for an envelope manufacturing plant. The company he worked for had turned down an order from Hallmark Cards that required special paper and new machinery. Harry learned about the order, purchased the special paper and with two employees, working in his garage, made the envelopes by hand. That was the origin of Midwest Envelope Company. Thanks primarily to Hallmark's loyalty, Midwest's exponential growth was such that the Navran family was never aware that the country was in a depression. After Southwest High, Jeane attended the University of Missouri for several semesters, but dropped out because the classes were "too boring". She returned to Kansas City and enrolled at the Kansas City Art Institute, where she found fulfillment for her artistic talents and the need for self expression.

Another pleasant surprise greeted me in Des Moines, my youngest sister, Eskie, was to be married to Mickey Engman. It was my good luck to be there to give the bride away. And what a perfect excuse to invite Jeane to Des Moines! And she accepted! Wow! That was the start of something big!

The six Navran siblings.

Shortly a;ter I returned to Mare Island, the destroyer we were waiting to be completed was sidetracked because o; a priority given to building a modern type light cruiser. I was reassigned to the USS John Rogers, a destroyer at sea. A;ter a short stint, I was trans;erred to the Gunnery O;;icers' School at Hickam Field, Hawaii, and upon graduation, assigned to the destroyer, the USS Wedderburn, as an assistant gunnery o;;icer.

Destroyers are designed to per;orm a variety o; duties, including escort duty to provide protection ;or battleship and aircra;t carrier groups against air, sea and submarine attacks; remote picket deployment to ;irst detect incoming kamikaze planes; close-in shore bombardments preceding army and marine landing cra;t invasions; to pursue and launch torpedoes against enemy sur;ace ships and, by sonar, seek and destroy with depth charges enemy submarines.

We were at sea ;or long stretches o; time without land sightings, thus mail deliveries were irregular. Some sixty ;ive years later, I still have recollections o; how I looked ;orward to the mail delivery o; Jeane's warm, humorous letters, many with clever hand drawn cartoons. They made my day....week.... month, until the next delivery.

Although we encountered the Japanese ;leet and aircra;t several times at various places, our ship emerged relatively unscathed ;rom battle damage. Our most damaging enemy turned out to be the ;ierce energy o; Mother Nature. A typhoon in the South China Seas swept through the Seventh Fleet causing unbelievable destruction and death. Mountainous waves capsized three destroyers and all aboard were lost; the cruiser Pittsburgh broke in two parts, the watertight compartments o; the bow heading in a di;;erent direction ;rom the rest o; the ship; an aircra;t carrier's deck was buckled like a washboard.

August 6, 1945, I happened to be on duty as the daily rotational o;;icer-o;-the-deck. I was handed a cable ;rom our ship's communication center, which I quickly ;orwarded to the captain. The captain read the contents o; the cable over the loud speaker: "NOW ALL HANDS HEAR THIS! AN ATOMIC BOMB HAS BEEN DROPPED ON HIROSHIMA". Pandemonium broke loose. Shortly therea;ter Japan surrendered and we made preparations to return home. On Navy Day, October 27, 1945, our ship was part o; the ;leet that dropped anchor in Boston Harbor. Jeane was on the dock to meet me.

Please meet me in Boston, Navy Day, 1945

Chapter 3
IN BOSTON EVEN BEANS DO IT –
LET'S FALL IN LOVE[1]

The sight of Jeane waving at me from the dock was a magical moment. As I walked down the gangplank to meet her, that "I'm-here-smile" buckled my knees (I'm sure it wasn't my sea legs that caused it).

Winding our way to the Commons, we devoured the beauty of that late autumn day. The week we spent in Boston was paradise found. We visited historical landmarks and museums, shopped at Faneuil Market, dined on fresh lobster at a dockside restaurant, toured Cape Ann while the last remnants of the color change clung to trees. We rocked at the Boston Pops concert and were able to get tickets to the wildly popular pre-Broadway showing of Oklahoma.

The chain hoisted anchor, and our ship departed for the Charleston Naval Base, to be decommissioned. The chain that bound the two of us that week in Boston, however, remained strong for over sixty-two years of married life.

---

[1] Excerpted from the lyrics of Cole Porter's song, "Let's fall in love".

Chapter 4
LOVE AND MARRIAGE
1946

I can't remember the circumstance under which I unofficially popped the question to Jeane, but I do recall the circumstance leading up to my formal request to her father for her hand in marriage.

S hortly after re-entering civilian life I was a guest at the home of Jeane's parents, Harry and Jennie Navran. At dinner that evening, prepared and served by her mother Jenny, were her brothers Bob and Dick, her father Harry, and Jeane and me. Midge, back in Kansas City, married to her lifelong sweetheart, Jerome Grossman (forget the brief fling with Floyd), came to visit us after dinner. Earlier in the day her mother, Jennie, asked if I had any preference for dinner. I assured her that inasmuch as I had been in the navy four years, anything would be a feast. As politely as I can put it, it was an interesting dinner. Brothers Bob and Dick and father Harry were each served different meals, like at a short order restaurant. Jeane was incensed. Not being one who keeps her feelings inside, she expressed her outrage at the men folks' dinner table demands. "If it were up to me", Jeane berated them, "I'd tell all of you to stop at a take-out counter and bring your own dinners home".

After dinner that evening, Jerome took me aside to warn me that marrying a Navran was a high maintenance undertaking, mentioning that when he approached Midge's father to ask for her hand in marriage, Harry thanked him profusely. The inevitable time came when I had to make my move. I asked Harry for a private meeting, to which he agreed, "Fine, around eight tonight in my study". I arrived punctually at his study, where he and Jerome were playing cards. Barely acknowledging that I was there, Harry motioned for me to pull up a chair. I sat. I waited and waited and waited. The card game ended around ten. Harry got up, thanked me for coming, and retired for the night.

I returned to Des Moines and investigated a couple of business opportunities that didn't work out. Meanwhile, at that time Jerome was an executive with Helzberg's, a fast growing regional jewelry store chain. He suggested that there might be a future for me with Helzberg's. I had never been inside a jewelry store (I bought Jeane's engagement ring at a ship's store), but I did have retail selling experience working part time in a men's clothing store while attending Drake

University. I applied for a sales job at Helzberg's Des Moines store, figuring that even if there was no future in it for me, the worst that could happen was that it would give me breathing space until something better came along.

Before the advent of bank credit cards, there was a category of jewelry stores, including Helzberg's, known as credit jewelers, where, in addition to diamonds, watches and jewelry, you could buy almost anything – dinnerware, silverware, gifts, housewares, small appliances, radios, record players and records, cameras -- for a dollar down and a dollar a week. As a sales clerk in a credit jewelry store, product knowledge was not a requirement. Here are two examples from my first few days. (As you may or may not know, most retail stores, including Helzberg's, that employ sales clerks who work on commissions, offer "push money" incentives to sell selected items that they are stuck with. These "push money" items were referred to as "spiffs".):

1. A farmer (recognizable by his overalls and sunburned face) came in to buy a watch for himself. I showed him a watch that was tagged with a coded $5.00 spiff. I asked if that was like something he had in mind. "Gee", he replied,

"that is really a spiffy looking watch". I assured him it was the spiffiest watch we had.

2 Helzberg's huge success was based on their marketing strategy of selling only "Certified Perfect Diamonds". The second day on the job I met my friend Billy Joseph for lunch. Billy worked in his father's store, Joseph Jewelers, a long established traditional "Tiffany" type store. Billy asked what I thought of the jewelry business. "I like it", I replied, "I sold a diamond ring today". After I revived him from shock, he asked what I knew about diamonds. "Nothing", I confessed, "but that isn't necessary. This guy came in to look at bridal sets. Before I showed him anything I read him the Certified Perfect Diamond Certificate, which guarantees, 'The center diamond in this bridal set is of fine color, of good cut and proportions and free from flaws or imperfections of any kind'. Next I asked if he preferred the Perfect $100 set, the Perfect $200 set or the Perfect $300 set. He said he wanted to spend around $200. I removed the set from the show case, showed it to him, and wrote up the sales ticket".

Actually, I did like the jewelry business. Jeane and I were married July 6, 1946. I was bringing home enough money to enable us to live reasonably well. We were able to make a down payment on a $15,000.00 government insured house in a reasonably good neighborhood. On today's market, it would probably be around an affordable $200,000 house. The house came with a garage, but we had not yet scraped up enough for a down payment on a car. Not only that, compared to these days when dealers are having trouble giving cars away, it may be hard to believe that back then, unless you had an uncle in the business, you were put on a wait list to buy a car but were never called unless you secretly agreed to pay the dealer hundreds of dollars cash "under the table".

July 6, 1946

Chapter 5
A TYPICAL AMERICAN S7 CCESS STORY

I stayed w8h Helzberg's and 8n 1948 we moved to Kansas C8y. Through Jeane's dad's ;r8endsh8p w8h a Chevrolet dealer we were able to purchase a new car w8hout pay8ng cash under the table. A cup o; co;;ee cost 5¢. Our ;8st born, W8l8am J., arr8ved August 7, 1949. I was promoted to ass8stant manager 8n one o; Helzberg's stores. It was the ;8st small step up the corporate ladder. I worked harder, arr8ved at work earl8er and stayed later; cons8stently won sales contests; created attract8ve w8ndow d8splays; kept the 8nventory pol8shed and the store as clean as poss8ble 8n ant8c8pat8on o; unannounced 8nspect8ons by company execut8ves. I ;elt con;8dent 8 was just a matter o; t8me be;ore a b8g break would come my way.

The b8g break came! Jeane's uncle Sam d8ed and le;t an 8nher8tance o; $5,000.00 to each o; h8s n8eces and nephews. Jeane and I started mak8ng plans to buy a jewelry store. I stopped 8n the co;;ee shop next door on my co;;ee break. The pr8ce o; co;;ee had gone up to 10¢ a cup. I was shocked and angry. I told the lady who owned the shop that she m8ght as well close up because nobody 8s ever go8ng to pay 10¢ ;or a cup o; co;;ee.

Leon Meyer, owner of Meyer Wholesale Jewelry, a supplier to jewelry stores throughout Kansas and Missouri, was a friend of Jeane's dad whom we prevailed upon for help in our search for a jewelry store to buy. Leon had in mind the right store for us to contact, Conklin Jewelers in Chanute, Kansas. Eugene Conklin was more or less bedridden and his wife, Marie, who ran the store, was anxious to retire. Their one son was a doctor, practicing in Dubuque, Iowa. One Sunday, Jeane and I met with Marie in Chanute. The store was established in 1890 and reeked of tradition. We loved the store. Marie loved us. Half of Jeane's inheritance was sufficient for a down payment. We bought the store.

Conklin Jewelers, Chanute, 1952

Chapter 6
AN IDEAL WIFE

Chanute is a town with a population of about 10,000 in Southeast Kansas, a two hour drive from Kansas City via US 169. The physical transplant to Chanute was relatively easy. We moved from a rented furnished apartment in Kansas City to a rented furnished home. Business was everything we had hoped for. I joined the Junior Chamber of Commerce, played golf, and even found time to take flying lessons. In that context, it appeared to me that it is easier for transplanted men to adapt to a new environment than it is for women, thus, I worried about Jeane. Her background did not prepare her for living in a small town. She didn't play golf or cards. She left behind her world of family and lifelong friends. By nature, Jeane was a fun loving party girl who attended ballet, opera, the theatre and symphonic concerts. For practical purposes, all of the above were out of reach. It turned out that my worries were for naught. Jeane blended in with extraordinary resilience, juggling to take care of Bill and to work in the store (excellent saleslady), and to make many new friends.

J eane returned to Kansas City in August of 1953 to give birth to Jim. For some time I had been thinking about surprising her by upgrading the engagement diamond that I had purchased at the ship's store. Conklin's diamond supplier was C. A. Kiger, a Kansas City firm. What better time to surprise her than when she was in the hospital? With four-year old son Bill in tow, we paid a visit to C. A Kiger's headquarters. Seated in a private room, I told their sales rep that I was interested in a two-carat round diamond. He ignored my request and proceeded to dump loose diamonds on the table. There lay diamonds of every shape, -- rounds, pears, marquises, emerald cuts, and ovals -- in every size, up to six carat. The sales rep explained, "this is just a sample of our inventory. I want you to remember us when you get a call for bigger diamonds than you carry in stock". It was mind boggling. I asked Bill what he thought about the multi-million dollar display of diamonds on the table. He wasn't impressed. "They're so little", he replied. We got back to reality, picked out a two-carat diamond and returned to the hospital to lighten Jeane's ordeal with our surprise.

Jeane went through the childbirth ordeals with both boys very well. It was me that our friends and relatives were concerned about. At the birth of Bill it seems that I conked out at the time of delivery and had to be revived by Jerome to learn that I was a father of a baby boy and that mother and son were doing well. I am happy to report that I survived the birth of Jim without incident.

Chapter 7
FAMILY MATTERS

After twin brother Louis's discharge from the air force, while contemplating his future, he temporarily went to live with our sister Dorothy, also a twin, in Peoria. That's right, there were two sets of twins in our family, Dorothy and Nettie, followed three years later by Louis and Harold. Early on we had our claim to fame when Flynn Milk Company ran our pictures in Sunday's photo gravure section of the Des Moines Register & Tribune, boasting that "These two healthy sets of twins are raised on Flynn's milk". Esther (Eskie) joined our family as a single seven years after the last set of twins.

Two consecutive sets of twins was a thought provoking topic of conversation. As it was told to me not long ago by my nephew Arnie, my dad, who had a reputation as a storyteller, was asked by a friend how to go about having twins. *"Here's what you do", dad advised, "Buy your wife a bewitching negligee, fragrant bath salts and a 'come hither' perfume. After she has bathed, perfume sprayed, and slipped into her negligee, call me".*

These two healthy sets of twins are raised on Flynn's Milk

Dorothy dropped out of the University of Illinois to marry her high school sweetheart, Hy Markman. The Markman clan were known as potato kings, with farms in Idaho and Bakersfield, California. Three Markman brothers independently owned the distribution offices in Des Moines, Davenport and Peoria. Hy owned the Peoria branch. After the war, brother Louis went to Peoria to visit Dorothy and Hy and stayed to work for a friend, Sol Rosenberg, who owned several ladies-ready-to-wear stores in the Peoria area. The plot thickens, dear reader, so pay attention. Sol's wife, Evelyn, was an aunt of Marilyn Bothman, an Ann Arbor beauty queen sought after by the Jewish frat boys at the University of Michigan. During a visit to Peoria to spend time with Sol and Evelyn, Marilyn and Louis met. Bingo! They married and moved to Ann Arbor, where Louis went to work in his father-in-law's ladies' sportswear store, named "The Marilyn Shop".

Our son Bill was born at the time of Marilyn's and Lou's wedding, thus we were unable to attend. Inasmuch as Jeane and I had not yet met Marilyn, Dorothy later invited the four of us to meet in Peoria, about half way between Ann Arbor and Chanute. We drove, arriving in Peoria before

Louis and Marilyn, who took the Rock Island Rocket from Chicago.

Louis and I were considered identical twins. Growing up, there were some comical incidents when our identities were inadvertently mixed up, but we never planned an incident. Hy, on the other hand, was a practical joker. His scheme was, when we met them at the train station, to hustle Marilyn to the back seat of his car and to hustle Louis in the train station to collect their luggage. I, not Louis, would emerge from the station and sit beside Marilyn in the back sat of Hy's car. Things worked out as he had planned. When I settled in the back seat of the car, here is how the conversation went:

MARILYN: I wonder if Jeane and Harold are in.

ME: I don't know.

MARILYN: Too bad Howie isn't in town.

ME: Yeah.

MARILYN: I'm anxious to see Sol's new store.

ME: Me, too.

Pause, at which time Marylyn brushes her hand against my coat.

MARILYN: shrieking: **You're not Louis.**

ME: I know it. How did you know?

MARILYN: *hysterical:* **Louis was wearing his cashmere coat. Your coat is not cashmere.**

I slink out of Hy's car and go back to my car:
JEANE: It was a lousy idea. You shouldn't
have done it.
ME: I know it.
I have the feeling that as long as she lived,
Marilyn thought I was weird.

Chapter 8
THE WANDERING JEWELER
1954

Traveling salesmen were not only purveyors of merchandise, they were purveyors of gossip as well. The gossip circulating around the territory was that Leben Jewelry in El Dorado (Kansas) was up for sale, the reason being that Ted Leben, the owner, who had been dabbling in oil as a part time venture, had hit it big. The significance of that rumor was these same gossipers had always portrayed Leben's the as one of the best jewelry stores in the area.

At that same time, Jeane inherited more money. Things were going reasonably well in Chanute, but the confluence of Jeane's inheritance and the sale of Leben's Jewelry induced in me dreams of grandeur. To shorten the story, we bought Leben's and soon thereafter bought a home in Wichita, a 25-minute commute on the turnpike from El Dorado.

The following year, our manager at Conklin's quit and we were unable to hire an affordable qualified manager. Sales plummeted. I fed the information to the traveling gossipers that Conklin's was for sale, but without success, so I decided to close it out. My hands were full at Leben's and Jeane's hands were full with the kids, so I contacted a liquidation firm to run a Store Closing Sale. To shorten the story again, I was disappointed in the way the sale was being handled and sent the liquidator's representative packing. I finished the liquidation sale myself.

At a meeting of the Kansas Retail Jewelers Association, Sam Hankins, a jeweler in Newton, just down the road a piece, mentioned to me that he was having a tough time paying his bills and needed to raise cash. I said, "Say no more, Sam, I am a veteran at running cash raising sales and will handle it for you. My fee will be 10% of net sales during the sale period". Sam must have been desperate because he agreed to give it a try.

The sale was a success. The traveling salesmen's gossip mills went into high gear. The next week I received a call to run a sale for Meador's, a fine jeweler in Hutchinson. Dear reader, I don't want to burden you with unknown names and places so I will compress the next ten years by saying that, without spending one cent to advertise my service, I personally prepared and conducted 103 sales – Store Closing Sales, Stock Reduction Sales, Retirement Sales, Store

34

Moving Sales, Grand Opening Sales, Anniversary Sales, Fire Sales, Lost Our Lease Sales, Partnership Dissolution Sales, Special Purchase Sales, Out-of-Season sales and Name-Your-Own-Reason-Sales[1].

---

[1] See NOTES, Chapter 0i , "Sales Promotions"

Chapter 9
WICHITA DAZE
1955

A CONDENSED HISTORY OF
OF JUDAISM'S FIRST 6,000 YEARS

We were happy to be back to city living. We joined the Jewish temple, the first time in our married life that we were members of a religious congregation. Wichita was populated with about 150 Jewish families, pretty evenly divided between memberships in the Reform Temple and the Conservative Synagogue. Many non-Jews think of Jewish people as a monolithic group. It's not even close to that. The spectrum of religious observance runs from the Reform prayer service, conducted 98% in English and so attuned to its congregants' assimilation, to the Orthodox prayer service, conducted 100% in Hebrew. The beards and unmistakable dress code of the Orthodox men are badges of their devotion to the immutable words of the Old Testament. Except for members of diamond bourses, Orthodox men are oblivious to their environment. Orthodox women are more difficult to visually identify, but the trail of children that walk behind them denotes their years of marriage. Conservative congregations are amalgamations of both the Reform and the Orthodox, but avoid the extremes.

*L*et me explain a practical difference between the three. A young man bought a thoroughbred racehorse, but before testing its full capabilities, he wanted to have the horse blessed, or as they say in Jewish, have a brachah (a blessing, pronounced bra-chah) said over the horse. He went to his orthodox rabbi to ask for the brachah (blessing). The rabbi said it was an unusual request, but he was willing to try to find a precedent that would grant him the authority to say the brachah (blessing). He reported back that no such authority could be found. Not discouraged, the young man went to the Conservative rabbi and asked for a brachah (blessing) to be said over his thoroughbred race horse. The rabbi said the request was beyond his authority to grant; the decision must be made by the Synagogue's Board of Directors. Because of the potential insurance liability, the board rejected the request. As a last resort, the young man went to the Reform Temple rabbi to ask for the brachah (blessing). The rabbi got quite excited about the horse, asking all kind of questions about its sire and dam, its racing performance under various track conditions, the veterinarian's report, and other esoteric questions. "By the way, young man", the Reform rabbi asked, "what's a brachah?"[1]

---

[1] See GLOSSARY, "Brachah" (Blessing).

Another misunderstanding about Jews is that anti-Semitism is attributed only to blatant, uncouth skin-heads and to the subtle country club phenomena. Again, dear reader, it isn't so. Sometimes Jews will behave like other Jews are their worst enemies. Let me give you an example:

In Wichita, A serious confrontation erupted when a member of the Synagogue came to a Friday night service at the Temple wearing a yarmulke, a skullcap worn by men and boys adhering to Conservative and Orthodox Judaism. The wearing of the yarmulke was an affront to many of our reform temple members. I am not making this up, a special board meeting was called to resolve the problem. Mature, successful men and women were having a serious debate about what punitive action should be taken to rectify this perceived insult. Countless hours of research were spent to find a precedent pertaining to the wearing of a yarmulke. None was found. It was concluded that, like the fiddler on the roof, the wearing of a yarmulke was a tradition that evolved without explanation. The matter was resolved by permitting the yarmulke to be worn at temple services, but with the understanding that the wearing of a yarmulke is not a tradition acceptable by our temple board.

Jeane and I were born Jews, but that's where our affiliation to Judaism ended. Jeane's parents were non-observing Reform Temple members. She attended Sunday school for its secular activities, and was Confirmed, whatever that meant. My parents belonged to a Conservative Synagogue. I went to Sunday school where I was taught the stories about Jonah and the whale, Methuselah and other "it ain't necessarily so" fables. At twelve years of age, Louis and I attended Hebrew school to learn to read (not understand) Hebrew in preparation for our Bar Mitzvahs, the ritual that we enter as boys and finish as men.

Hebrew school classes were held at the Jewish Community Center, where the facilities included an indoor basketball court and an outdoor playing field suitable for baseball, soccer and football games. After public school classes, three times a week, Louis and I would board a street car that would dump us at the Center about an hour before our class was scheduled to begin. The standard operating procedure was at class time the rabbi would drag us from the playing field or basketball court, depending on the season, to the classroom. Dear reader, I must now ask you to accompany me on a fast forward trip to when Louis is living in Ann Arbor, a suburb of

Detroit, and a Hebrew school classmate, Max Steinway, is living in Detroit. They renewed their past Hebrew school friendship. Louis and Marilyn, and Max and his wife were invited to attend the Bar Mitzvah of a son of a mutual friend. Louis flat-out refused to go, so Marilyn attended the ceremony with Max and his wife. Reading Hebrew from a sacred scroll is an important part of the Bar Mitzvah ritual. As the Bar Mitzvah boy was reading Hebrew, Max, seated beside Marilyn, was silently accompanying him. At the conclusion of the ceremony, Marilyn said to Max, "It's amazing that you've retained Hebrew well enough to go through the ceremony by rote, but Louis can't read one word in Hebrew". "There is one thing you must understand, Marilyn", Max replied, "Louis went through Hebrew school on an athletic scholarship".

THE GOLF TOUR

When we joined Rolling Hills Country Club, the membership was approximately 10% Jewish, 90% Gentile. Jeane planned many of our social events around the Sunday night dinners at the club. One Saturday night Jeane and I were invited by a golfing buddy to a party at the club. The club manager spotted Jeane and spoke to her of his frustration: "This would be a better club", he confided, "if you could get some of your Jewish friends to come here and drink with us on Saturday nights and I could get some of these goyem (i.e. Gentiles) to come to Sunday night dinners and enjoy eating like you Jewish people".

❁

The mixed membership clubs, like Rolling Hills, were a reminder that many clubs were still segregated -- no Jews or Negroes allowed. Brother Louis and his golfing foursome traveled on golf outings to various country clubs around the country. Louis called the prestigious Greenbrier Golf and Country Club in Virginia for a tee time reservation, giving the clerk at the reservation desk the names of the foursome, Louis Oppenheim, Bob Sandler, Lester Bookey and Max Steinway. The reservation clerk asked if any of the foursome was Jewish. "No suh, boss", Louis replied, "we is all niggers".

Which reminds me of another of Louis's (non ethnic) golf stories. Their foursome arranged a starting time at the newly opened Doral Country Club in Miami. Bob Sandler, a member of the foursome, had been in an automobile accident when he was nine years old that resulted in the amputation of his right arm above the elbow. Bob developed unbelievable strength and agility in his left arm, to become captain of the 7ni versity of Iowa tennis team, and later went on to win an International Amputees' Golf Tournament. The "Blue Monster" golf course at Doral was open but some of the clubhouse facilities were not. As Bob was leaving the clubhouse, a golfer entering it asked him if the barber shop was open. "It's open", Bob cautioned, "but whatever you do, don't get a manicure".

THE OIL BOOM

Socially, we were in touch with some of Wichita's oil producers . By the nature of the business, you can safely assume that oil men are gamblers. One night the topic of conversation was that the price of oil had pretty much stabilized at around $1.70 a barrel. One oilman proposed to wager that the price would hit $2.00 before it dropped to $1.50. He had a taker. That was back in 1955, so forgive me if I can't remember who won the bet.

HOW TO LOSE FRIENDS
AND ALIENATE PEOPLE

At the age of three, we noticed that Jim had some skin irritations and was scratching himself a lot. Jeane made an appointment with Dr. Lazar, an allergist. Because getting a sitter for Bill was not a practical option, Jeane took Bill, then aged seven, with her to the doctor's office. After the usual paper work and delay, a nurse came and grabbed Bill and took him into the inner office. Alarmed, Jeane went to the reception desk to tell the receptionist that the nurse had taken the wrong boy. The receptionist went in the inner office and reported back that the doctor was examining the patient and she couldn't interfere. When the nurse emerged with Bill, she handed Jeane several prescriptions for allergy medication for him, with instructions that included reporting back to Dr. Lazar for bi-weekly testing. After completion of Jim's examination, Jeane protested to Dr. Lazar that Bill had no allergy problem, that he was with her only because she couldn't get a sitter for him. Dr. Lazar was unrelenting. He insisted that Bill start taking the medication immediately and report back to see him in two weeks for further testing.

When I came home from work, Jeane, still shook up, told me the horror story. The following day I phoned Dr. Lazar to inform him of the mistake. In no way was I going to have Bill's prescriptions filled or make an office appointment. The following is the gist of the conversation:

DR. LAZAR: Are you telling me that I don't know my business?

ME: No. I said your nurse made a mistake.

Dr. LAZAR: The boy has allergies that need attention.

ME: He didn't have them before you saw him.

DR. LAZAR: I don't have time for this conversation. Click. The phone went dead.

44

Chapter 10
MESH7 GA[1] IN MIAMI
1957

This is an X rated chapter filled with strong adult language and sex smut. Persons 18 years old or younger must skip this chapter, except those who have served in Bush's war in Iraq.

As Jerome continued his ascent up the corporate ladder at Helzberg's, one of his perks was a two week vacation at the boss's winter home in Bal Harbor, an upscale enclave between the Miami mainland and Miami Beach, complete with a car with a rumble seat[2] and with a guest cabana at a luxury beachfront hotel. The perk entitled him to invite house guests to share his vacation. Naturally, Jeane and I were overjoyed to receive the invitation.

We emplaned midst the wicked winter winds of Wichita and deplaned inhaling Miami's balmy fragrance. We were picked up at the airport by Jerome and Midge and taken to Junior's, a famous Miami Beach deli. My corned beef sandwich was one inch thick. At the deli I was beginning

---

[1] Jewish for crazy.
[2] An uncovered seat that opened from the rear of the 1933 vintage Chevrolet.

to feel that I had returned to the land of my people. That feeling was reinforced the next morning while I was sunning myself on the Helzberg dock. A boy of about ten appeared out of nowhere to join me. "What's your name?" I asked. "Guess" he replied. The conversation continued like this:

ME: I'm no good at guessing.

BOY: I'll give you a hint. It's the most popular name at my school.

ME: Tom Brown? Jim Jones?

BOY: No.

ME: I give up. What is it?

BOY: David Cohen.

Later that day, the girls dropped Jerome and me at the Normandy Isle Golf Club, a public course on Miami Beach, and went on to do their thing. There was a waiting list for a tee-off time. I had incontestable proof that I was in the land of my people when the starter introduced us to a guy named Harold Friedman, who would join us. "What a coincidence" I remarked, "I have a friend in Des Moines named Harold Friedman". "So what's the big coincidence", he growled, "on Miami Beach alone there are six Harold Friedmans".

When we returned to the clubhouse after our round of golf, we joined the girls at a table where they were having drinks. Jeane giggled, "You must try this new drink Midge introduced me to. It's called a Bloody Mary. It has a great taste and you don't even that know you've been drinking". Being a scotch drinker, I declined. A drink or two later, when we decided to leave, Jeane's knees buckled and we had to prop her up to keep her from falling.

The next day the routine was the same: the girls dropped us off at Normandy Isle and went on to do their thing. When we met them after golf at their table, Jeane was sober this time, but bubbly. "Midge and I found a shoe store on Lincoln Road that you can't believe", she bubbled. Inasmuch as Jeane was a scratch[1] shopper, I believed her. She may not have been in Imelda Marcus's class, but Jeane did have a shoe fetish. Her discovery reminded me of a joke that I kept to myself because Jeane was certain that I have a warped sense of humor. *There was this girl drooling at a shoe store window, muttering to herself that she would do anything to be able to afford the pair of shoes in the window. A gentlemen standing nearby*

---

[1] Synonym for a golfer who shoots par, i.e. "scratch golfer".

happened to overhear her muttering and approached to ask, "Excuse me, m'am, did you say 'anything'?" Oh, yes", she sighed, "anything". He offered her the price of the shoes in exchange for her services. She demurred, "It's a generous offer, sir, but I'm afraid I would disappoint you. I'm not the least bit passionate". "My offer stands", he insisted. It was a deal. As her services were in progress, she tightly squeezed her arms and legs around him. Delighted, he whispered, "why did you lie to me when you said you weren't passionate? "Forget it", she replied, "I'm trying on my new shoes".

One morning Jerome saw an ad in the Miami Herald that Tony Martin was the star attraction at the Beachcomber night club on the beach. Major Grossman reminisced that Sergeant Martin was on his staff in India during WW II. He made a dinner reservation at the Beachcomber that night. When we arrived, Jerome handed the maitre d´ a note informing Tony that Major Grossman was there and would like to see him. During a break after his first performance, Tony came to our table, bear-hugged Jerome and spent the next half hour or so telling interesting stories of his career on stage, in movies and as a recording artist. I was hoping he would comp the dinner, but no such luck. (Tony had a recent performance with good reviews at the Regency Hotel in New York City in 2007, then at the age of 95).

48

Foul mouthed Belle Barth was a "must see" performer at her own nightclub, Belle's Barthroom in Miami Beach. Before relating our soiree at the Barthroom, however, we must start with a flashback. Early on in our married lives, when Jeane and I double dated with Madge and Jerome, the conversation inexorably turned to either Helzberg's or sex. On the latter topic, Jerome once made a big deal out of his observation that Madge was more fully endowed, bosom-wise, than Jeane. I'm sure you know what I mean. Fast forward to Belle's Barthroom. It was structured like a miniature football stadium. Customers entering the room like players enter the playing field from the locker room passageway. The audience was seated in an elevated circular arrangement that enabled everyone to witness all of the comings and goings at the club. Belle was enthroned on high, playing her piano and jabbering. When the four of us entered the club, she stopped playing the piano and greeted us. Belle said to Jeane, "Honey, I love your yellow dress. Yellow is my favorite color. My house is yellow, my car is yellow, my toilet paper is yellow". After a brief pause, she added, "but your tits are small", to which Jeane blurted, "That's what my brother-in-law told me". Jeane's reply brought down the house. When the laughter eventually subsided, Belle gave

Jeane some advice, "To hell with your brother-in-law", she counseled, "if it keeps your husband happy, that's all that matters".

Patsy Abbott was another chanteuse entertaining at a night club on Miami Beach. She didn't interact with audiences like Belle Barth, but she told some good off-color jokes. My favorite was the story about the Catholic lady and the Jewish lady who were educating each other about their respective religions. *The Catholic lady went first, explaining the significance of the icons and rituals, and the meaning of important holidays. The Jewish lady told her about our most important holidays: "Passover, celebrating the end of Jewish bondage in Egypt, Rosh Hashanah, celebrating the New Year, and Yom Kippur, a day of atonement, when we Jews ask God to forgive us of our sins. The blowing of a ram's horn, in Hebrew called a shofar, a high pitched toot...toot...toot that punctuates each sin we confess to (our sins are conveniently listed for us in the prayer book). We then spend time confessing our sins, each confession followed by the blowing of the shofar". The Catholic lady smiled and said, "that's what I like about you Jewish ladies, you're always so good to your help".*

Our routine was that the girls would pick up Jerome and me late every afternoon at Normandy Isle, have a few drinks for the road, and drive home. The route took us past a steak house with a huge flashing electric sign, "SIRLOIN STEAK, $2.79". This was 1957, but $2.79 was el cheapo for a sirloin steak dinner even then. As early as 5:00 there would be a block-long line waiting to get in. The day before our scheduled return home, curiosity prevailed and we decided to stand in the dinner line. It was really slow-moving. What seemed like ages later we got close enough to the entrance for me to ask the big dude guarding the door how long it would be before we would be seated. He didn't answer me, but turned to the diners inside and in a bullhorn voice answered, **"As soon as some of these yokels finish drinking their coffee, I'll have a place for you"**. Actually, the steaks weren't bad and the service was unhurried. We didn't stay for the coffee.

51

At the Beachcomber with Tony Martin, who served in the army with Major Grossman in India.

Chapter 11
MIAMI BEACH REVISITED

THE CRYSTAL HO7 SE
1963

Sister Nettie's life was shattered and all of her Sioux City friends went into shock when her marriage to Morris Lasensky broke up. A friend and neighbor of theirs was convicted of fraudulent dealings with the government and sentenced to jail. Before leaving, the neighbor asked Morris to look in on his wife from time to time to make sure that she was o.k. I'm sure, dear reader, you have guessed the finish of the story. Morris and the neighbor's wife obtained divorces from their respective spouses, cut all ties and presumably lived happily ever after in California.

Thankfully, time can heal a broken heart. Nettie met and married a retired widower, Sol Brooks, living at the Crystal House, a prestigious apartment address on Miami Beach. Sol was legally blind with only peripheral vision, but always had a smile on his face and an upbeat manner. Sol's sister was married to Sidney Lipkins, owner of the Crystal House and of the 75-foot yacht anchored in the bay, across the street.

I didn't know much about Sidney's source of wealth other than it was attributed to his ownership of Broadway Maintenance, a firm reputed to be well connected in New York City politics. When Jeane and I arranged to meet Louis and Marilyn in Miami Beach, we were billeted in a guest apartment at the Crystal House.

Nettie was a classy lady. She had good looks, style, charm, warmth, a kind heart and was fun to be with. But Nettie wasn't perfect. She complained to her banker that her account in no way could be overdrawn because she still had plenty of checks left in her checkbook.

When it was not otherwise committed, Nettie and Sol had access to Sidney's yacht with its two-man crew. The yacht slept six passengers. Marilyn and Louis, Jeane and I were guests of Nettie's and Sol's on overnight intercoastal cruises to Key Largo, Boca Raton and Palm Beach. The standard operating procedure was that we would dock early in the afternoon at our destination, Louis and I would play golf, the girls would shop, we would all dine at a local restaurant, sleep on board, spend the morning at breakfast and sightseeing, return to the yacht and head back to the Crystal House.

A not-so-funny thing happened in Palm Beach. When we returned from our morning outing to head home, a gun-toting U. S. Marshal was standing guard at the entrance of the yacht and would not permit us to board. It seems that the yacht had undergone repairs and a lien for the unpaid bill had been placed against it. Sol was able to contact Sidney in New York to learn that Sidney considered the cost of the repairs outrageous and he had refused to pay it. Sidney apologized for the inconvenience but there was nothing he could do at the moment. We hired a limo and returned to the Crystal House, sans our overnight clothes and toiletries. So much for emulating the rich and famous.

At the Crystal House

Alongside Sidney's Yacht

Chapter 12
MIAMI BEACH REVISITED

BAY HARBOR
1966

Hy and Dorothy had retired and were living in Bay Harbor. Hy was sort of looking around for something to do and/or invest in. Before leaving Peoria, Dorothy was selling real estate and was sort of planning to restart a career in Miami. Dorothy had, and at age 93, still has, stunning good looks, a winning personality and the smarts. She was a debater on Roosevelt High School's championship debate team and, with partner Betty Butler, a finalist in the state women's tennis doubles championship.

As 1966 drew to a close, I was physically and mentally exhausted. Jeane decided the best thing for me, the boys and herself was to pack my things and send me somewhere for a week or two of rest. Dorothy and Hy graciously agreed to take me in.

Although rest and relaxation were my ostensible reason for revisiting Miami Beach, the thought of living there had been lying dormant in my brain's little grey cells since my first visit there almost a decade

58

before. When Hy and Dorothy were living in Peoria, I ran a jewelry store liquidation sale there. Hy, who was mostly retired at that time, worked pro bono for me at the store. He liked what he learned about the jewelry business during the sale[1]. Thus we had common ground: Hy with time and money to invest in a business he liked and I with the scheme of transplanting my business to the Miami area.

✿

Our wholesale/retail jewelry outlet store in Wichita had evolved into what had became known as a Catalog/Showroom. During a span of about four decades, starting in the late forties, Catalog/Showrooms were important retail outlets in almost all metropolitan areas[2].

Researching the entire Miami/Fort Lauderdale area disclosed that there was only one catalog/showroom in an area that could easily support one more. The

---

[1] While in Peoria, I stayed with Hy and Dorothy. Returning home at the completion of the sale, Dorothy took me to the airport in her car. I drove. We kissed goodbye and I boarded the plane with the keys to Dorothy's car in my pocket. Fortunately, flight control was able to abort the takeoff, enabling Dorothy to retrieve her car keys.

[2] See NOTES, Chapter 12, "Catalog/Showrooms"

remainder of my rest and relaxation time was spent with Hy searching for the right location. We bought a new 10,000 square foot building in North Miami Beach, not far from the new, highly successful enclosed 163rd Street Shopping Mall.

I returned home, tanned and rested, with a big surprise for Jeane: we were going to move to North Miami Beach. Knowing that sooner or later I would make my dream of year-round golf become a reality, it wasn't much of a surprise to her. She was, however, overjoyed that it was going to happen. She loved the beach and the shopping, but more importantly, looked forward to family life with Dorothy and Nettie, both of whom she loved.

Dorothy at 93

Nettie
Nov. 13, 1915 -- May 11, 1990

Chapter 13
O7 R PLACE IN THE S7 N
January, 1967

Since 1946 we had been living like gypsies, -- moving ;rom Des Moines to Kansas City to Chanute to El Dorado to Wichita. The contemplated move to Miami Beach, however, was envisioned as a ;inal destination. Another di;;erence about this move was that Bill and Jim were now teenagers, doing their own things. Bill, age 17, no longer living at home, was attending Wichita State 7 niversity; Jim, age 13, was in middle school. When we broke the news to them about our planned move, Bill bid us goodbye and good luck. He had no intention o; moving to Miami Beach with us. Jim, given no choice, resented our sel;ish lack o; consideration by making the decision to move without ;irst discussing it with him.

❋

Our country was being torn apart by the Vietnam war. The di;;erence between the war in Vietnam and the war in Iraq, is that during Vietnam every young man was eligible to be dra;ted in the army, whereas we have an all volunteer army in Iraq. One pro;ound e;;ect o; that di;;erence is that during Vietnam, college campuses were ri;e with student protests. It gave birth to the age of hippies.

Hippies were mostly peace-seeking pot smokers, identifiable by their anti-establishment attire and attitude. Bill was a hippie. His appearance and behavior were tolerable, but when he was caught smoking pot, I thought he crossed the line. Unfortunately, as a parent, I was not properly trained to deal with what I perceived to be a disciplinary problem. My solution was to punt the problem to a psychologist. After extracting enormous bribes from me, Bill agreed to meet with him. At the conclusion of his first (and only) session with the psychologist, I asked Bill how it went. "It was o.k.", he replied, "but that guy is in bad shape. He really needs help". Come July, we had wound up our affairs in Wichita and departed for Miami Beach with our maligned son, Jim, in tow.

Chapter 14
OPPENHEIM DISTRIB7 TORS
Catalog/Showroom
July, 1967

Dorothy had arranged for us to rent a 2-bedroom, 2-bath furnished apartment in the Sky Lake subdivision of North Miami Beach called the Presidential Gardens, not far from the building we had purchased for our catalog/showroom business. To Jeane it was regressive. She hated it. To Jim it was a community for the aged. He hated it. I thought it was o.k. Since my navy days, I had a tendency to look at everything through rose-colored glasses. Jeane's priority was to find more suitable living quarters. My concern was to get our business open as soon as possible.

Between June 1, the day we took possession of the building, and the day after Thanksgiving, the day we opened for business, we had hired our staff, had all fixtures and merchandise in place, and had mailed 25,000 catalogues to local businesses and professional people. The line of people waiting to get in on Opening Day was nearly a block long.

Dealing with the public isn't all fun and games, but there were some laughable moments, like the time a gentleman came in to look at diamond rings.

ME: Are you interested in an engagement ring, wedding ring or dinner ring?

CUSTOMER: (No answer).

ME: Do you have a price range in mind?

CUSTOMER: (No answer).

ME: (I showed him a dinner ring in the medium price range). This is one of our newest styles......

CUSTOMER: Do you have something better?

ME: (I showed him three more rings, each one higher in price, each time he never let me finish a sentence, each time he asked to see something better). Sir, this is the most expensive ring we have in stock, it's........

CUSTOMER: I'll take it. Now, I have to buy something for my wife. Do you carry the GE toaster ovens?

Herman, one of our sales associates, came to Miami from a fractious family jewelry store up north. It seems that he had serious disagreements with his wicked stepmother, who ran the store. His background check and polygraph test were clean. Herman sold a 14 karat gold bracelet watch to a lady who had a small wrist. Our jeweler was able to

65

resize the bracelet to fit, but instead of laying flat on her wrist, the buckle tilted slightly. She agreed to Herman's suggestion that we return the watch to the factory for correction. When we got the watch back, the correction did not satisfy the customer. "Madam", Herman asked, "Did it ever occur to you that there is nothing wrong with the bracelet, it's your wrist that's deformed?"

With much fanfare, 1847 Rogers Bros. introduced a new pattern of silverplated flatware named "Eternally Yours". I'm not sure what the lady had in mind when she stopped in the store and asked to see 1847 Rogers Bros.' new pattern, "Internally Yours".

We hired Mr. Fairman, a retired friend of the Markmans from Peoria, as a sales associate. He was so happy to have something to do, he would have gladly worked for nothing, but I prevailed upon him to accept $2.00 an hour. Once when I was otherwise occupied, I asked Mr. Fairman to handle a customer's complaint for me. I noticed that he and the complaining customer were carrying on like long lost friends. After the customer departed with a smile on her face, I spoke with Mr. Fairman:

ME: I was impressed with the way you handled the complaint. How do you do it?

MR. FAIRMAN: It's easy. It all goes in one ear and out the other.

From that day forward, all customer complaints were referred to the appropriately named Mr. Fairman.

❦

A bored, retired friend of mine decided to buy a bar and go back in business. He contacted a business broker who recommended a bar for sale on Miami Beach. Without disclosing his intentions, my friend visited the bar and ordered a scotch and soda. The bartender placed the drink on the counter.

BARTENDER: That will be four dollars.

My friend watched as the bartender rang up four dollars on the cash register but put two dollars in the register and two dollars in his pocket. My friend ordered another scotch and soda. The bartender placed the drink on the counter.

BARTENDER: That will be four dollars.

My friend watched as the bartender rang up four dollars on the cash register but put all four dollars in his pocket.

MY FRIEND: What's the problem, aren't we partners anymore?

The moral of that story is that in a cash flow business be prepared to have silent partners. Take, for instance, the story of Dick Webber.

Dick Webber, manager of our jewelry and watch department, came to us well recommended from Mayor's Jewelers, a prestigious regional chain. One of his duties was to take in jewelry repairs, advising the customer of the cost and delivery date of the repair. The less intricate repairs were done on-premises, the more intricate ones he sent to Davis Jewelry Repair, a trade shop in downtown Miami. A bonded and insured delivery service picked up and delivered customers' repair jobs on a twice-a-week route to and from downtown. There were, however, urgencies when Webber decided to deliver or pick up a repair job himself.

Webber had an office in our private jewelry and watch repair section. One day I went to his office to tell him that I had a dental appointment downtown and would stop by Davis to pick up any repairs that were urgently needed. Before I left, Hy, who was good at detective work, told me that he had eavesdropped on a phone conversation in which Webber said to Davis, "Don't say anything to Oppenheim". I hadn't the slightest clue as to what Davis wasn't to say to me, but that didn't deter me from trying to find out. "O.K.", I knowingly asserted to Davis, "The jig is up. You might want to fill me in with the details". Davis disclosed, in general, Webber's strange demands to finish many repair jobs while he waited. My later bluff elicited a full confession from Webber:

Webbber told me that he was in financial trouble, rooted in gambling debts. He concocted a variation of the Ponzi Scheme to keep afloat by pawning some of the completed customers' repair jobs instead of filling them with "Repair Jobs Completed". When a customer came in to pick up a repair job that had been pawned, Webber feigned calling Davis and told the customer it would ready the following day. Webber then went to the pawn shop with a different completed repair job, or jobs, of sufficient value to redeem the needed item. If the available repair jobs were inadequate, he simply "borrowed" an item of our inventory to pawn. A contrite Webber handed me twenty three unredeemed pawn tickets.

A shocking twist to his elaborate scheme was that the pawn receipts were issued by Westin Jewelers, at that time a reputable jewelry store in downtown

---

1 A Ponzischeme, named after the notoriously famous Charles Ponzi is a fraudulent investment operation that pays returns to investors from money paid in by subsequent investors rather than from any profits actually earned. The Ponzischeme has many variations.

Hollywood (Florida), owned by a respected Hollywood businessman. As many of my dear readers know, a person receiving stolen goods is as guilty as the person who stole them. Accompanied by my attorney, the police chief of North Miami Beach and the police chief of Hollywood, I presented Mr. Westin with 23 pawn receipts for stolen merchandise to be redeemed. Mr. Westin, of course, pleaded innocent of any wrongdoing, claiming that he thought Webber to be one of several jewelers he financed, using their pawned diamond and jewelry items as loan security. My attorney explained to Mr. Westin that he was not being accused of any wrongdoing, but nevertheless he was in possession of stolen merchandise and could avoid a lot of adverse publicity if he turned over to me, this moment, and without charge, the twenty three pawned items in exchange for the pawn receipts. Mr. Westin readily agreed.

Taking into consideration that Webber was forthcoming and truly contrite, and that his innocent wife and two lovely children would suffer irreparable harm, I decided not to pursue charges against him on his promise that he would never, ever seek employment in a jewelry store. He agreed to the condition. Would you believe, about six months later I received a call from Mayor's

Jewelry, Webber's former employer, asking for a recommendation in regard to Dick Webber. Go figure.

❧

Hy and Dorothy bought a condo at Palm Aire, a huge resort development in Pompano Beach that included four golf courses, a hotel and a world renowned spa. Hy decided that he preferred life as a golf and beach bum to working. Jeane and I bought his interest in Oppenheim Distributors. At Palm Aire, Dorothy eventually restarted her successful career of selling real estate

❧

We joined a buying group of independently owned catalog/showrooms. I was selected to be a member of the group's jewelry committee, which entailed a week in New York meeting with manufacturers' representatives to select diamond and jewelry items for the group's next year's catalogs. One of our prospective suppliers was Hammerman Brothers, an upscale jewelry manufacturer.

Dear reader, I must ask your indulgence while I digress to introduce my niece, Dorothy's and Hy's daughter, Valerie. She was – and at the age of 73, still is – a knockout. Valerie, at that time living in Fairfield, Connecticut, married to Larry Schwartz, a banker, epitomized the life style of the rich and famous. When I called her from New York to arrange a convenient place to meet, I gave her my schedule of the times and places where I would be. She chose to meet me at Hammerman Brothers' showroom.

When our committee arrived at Hammerman's showroom, Valerie, to the shock and awe of my committee members, greeted me with a hug and a kiss. With total disbelief in their faces, I introduced the group to my niece, Valerie. The general consensus was, "Uh-huh". At the ensuing meeting, our committee members were mostly consumed with speculating about whether Valerie was or was not really my niece.

A watch repairer's workplace is a jungle of electrical wires adjacent to containers of flammable fluids used in the cleaning and overhauling of watches. Early in November, 1913, an electrical spark jumped into a flammable container causing heavy black smoke and fire that rapidly engulfed the interior of our building. After calling the fire department, we evacuated the building. The fire department, just two blocks away, responded quickly, but extensive damage to merchandise and fixtures had been done by the smoke, fire and the fire department. There are bad jokes about business fires, but the most traumatic moments of my life were standing outside watching smoke and fire emanate from our building. We had purchased, paid for and just mailed 35,000 catalogs, at a cost of $1.85 each, that went down the toilet. The year's profit in the catalog/showroom business, dependent on a successful Christmas season, was wiped out.

The building was completely renovated by the insurer's contractor in the middle of February, 1974. The slow agony of reaching a settlement with the insurance adjuster on the replacement value of inventory, that was pretty much totaled except for some diamond and jewelry items that could be restored, and with customer's claims for items in for repair, was excruciating. Literally and figuratively, when the dust settled, Jeane and I were of the same mind: no more retail business. (More on that later).

Chapter 15
CANONGATE, THE EARLY DAYS
December, 1969

Jeane had been assiduously studying the real estate pages of the Miami Herald and making appointments with realtors to look at condominiums. While not exactly sure of what she did want, she was sure of what she did not want, -- an ocean front high rise with its congested traffic and overcrowded restaurants. We bought a three bedroom, two bath condominium at Canongate, with 2,000 square feet of enclosed living space and a generous patio, on the periphery of the newly completed Sky Lake Golf and Country Club, at a pre-construction price of $36,000.00.

Canongate was financed by the Teamsters Union's Central States Pension Fund, serious real estate developers in South Florida at that time. Uniquely, Canongate aspired to double as an investment and as a vacation home for the top echelon of Teamsters' executives. Red Strata was the resident sales manager at Canongate. After Jeane and I had made the decision to buy at Canongate, and Red had the papers prepared for us to sign, I mentioned to Red, that as a routine matter, I always ask my lawyer to review any document before I sign it.

"No problem", Red mumbled. After reviewing the papers, my lawyer's opinion was that they were standard Florida real estate documents that were o.k. to sign. He commented, however, that he would prefer that our deposit be placed in a separate escrow account instead of being co-mingled with the developer's general funds. We returned to close the deal, with the documents unsigned. I repeated my lawyer's comment about our deposit to Red. Not one prone to subtleness in resolving a difference of opinion, Red suggested, "Oppenheim, do me a favor. Tell your lawyer to drop dead". We signed the papers.

❁

Early on there were condo parties and group activities. It was like permanent resort living. One of the fun trips was to Disneyland. It was planned as a four-day outing, but three of us figured that three days of traipsing around the park was enough, so we packed our golf clubs. As planned, on the fourth day the three of us headed for the golf course. Leon Englesberg had enough too. He asked to join us but didn't bring his golf equipment. We went with him to the pro shop while he rented clubs and shoes and bought a golf shirt. He hesitated, however, about buying some golf balls. "If anyone has spare golf balls I can borrow", Leon suggested, "I will repay you when we return home". As it happened, I had an unopened box o; a dozen Titleists, the overwhelming choice o; gol; pro;essionals. I opened the box and handed him a package o; three balls. On the ;irst tee, Leon's ;irst drive went in the lake on the le;t; his second drive went deep in the woods on the right; the third landed in the creek that crossed the ;airway. Leon turned and asked me ;or another package o; balls. "Look, Leon", I protested, "These are brand new Titleists". Leon admonished me, "Harold i; you can't a;;ord gol; balls, you shouldn't be playing gol;".

On Valentine's Day in the mid-1970s, Irv Lichtman, a snow bird (winter resident) and owner o; a chain o; car care centers in the Bu;;alo area, stopped me as I was passing through Canongate's lobby. "Come outside with me", Irv requested, "I want to show you something". Irv had bought a ;ew pieces o; jewelry ;rom us in the past, so I thought he may have had a question about jewelry. We stopped next to a car in the parking lot. The transcript:

IRV: What do you think o; it?

ME: What do I think o; what?

IRV: This car.(The one we were standing next to). Dear reader, in order ;or the ;ollowing conversation to make sense, I'm going to update the dollar ;igures in terms o; today's prices, not what they actually were in the mid 1970s:

IRV: (continuing before I answered): It's a Rolls Royce Phantom with only 39,000 miles on it. It's like new, hardly broken in. It's going to be a Valentine present for Lenore. Rolls' suggested list price is $340,000, but it's a dealer's repossession I bought for the balance due of less than $200,000.

ME: That's great. I'm sure she'll love it. (Actually, the styling reminded me of an old 1949 Dodge. At that price, I thought the least the Rolls' people could have done was add a few strips of chrome. And a tail fin like the 1970s Cadillacs would have helped).

The following morning I had a golf date with three snowbirds from Buffalo, Irv, Jack Gelman and Leo Bitlikoff. At breakfast, Irv repeated the Rolls Royce story. Jack shook his head in disbelief. "Irv", Jack asked Irv seriously, "Why on earth would you buy a used car?"

Son Jim was given a 1965 Oldsmobile coupe to drive back and forth to attend Norland High School. Somewhere between Canongate and Norland High there was a very small town with a very alert policeman operating a very efficient radar gun aimed at all passing cars. After receiving his third speeding ticket, Jim and I were summoned to appear at a very small courthouse in that very small town. A very stern judge addressed Jim, saying, "Young man, you are a hellcat on wheels. $20.00. Case dismissed". Later, when a pickup truck crashed into him his Olds was totaled and he spent five days in the hospital. Unfortunately, those five days were during finals week, causing him to flunk some courses. With his insurance money he was able to buy an army type Jeep and be king of the road.

Jim had a friend his age, Benjy Lieberman, that turned out to be a beneficial relationship. One influence that had life altering relevance was Benjy's introduction of Jim to the spiritual and philosophical teachings of Avatar Meher Baba. Inspired to learn more, Jim made his first pilgrimage to India . (More on that later.) Back home, Jim had a penchant for the medical profession. His first job was as a respiratory therapist. Later, he chose chiropractic because he did not want to become a dispenser of pills.

As planned, some of the Teamsters' top brass showed up at Canongate. Two that I met were a Mr. Flynn from Cleveland and a Mr. Dorfman, the Teamsters' insurance broker from Chicago. Frank

Fitzsimmons, who became the Teamsters' President following the mysterious disappearance of Jimmy Hoffa, did stay in the building, but I never saw him. I heard, with disbelief, that Claire Bender, a resident, approached Mr. Fitzsimmons in the lobby and asked, "O.K., Frank, what did you do with the body?"

Chapter 16
SKY LAKE GOLF
AND COUNTRY CLUB

W e joined The Sky Lake Golf and Country Club. The unheard of thing about the Country Club was that for the first two years (until the club was sold) the liquor was free. It seems that the Florida authority that dispenses liquor licenses withheld a liquor license because the club ownership was tainted with a mafia connection. "To hell with it", exclaimed Mr. Russo, the executive director, "If we can't sell liquor, we'll give it away". What can I tell you? The club became a Mecca for its members, their relatives and friends, and friends of their relatives and friends of their friends, ad infinitum. . There was gourmet dinner and dancing every Saturday night. Entertainers on the condo circuit made regular appearances. An evening with Gordon MacRae (remember Curly in the musical film Oklahoma?) was one of the best. He had just come from a dinner celebration at Arnold Palmer's Bay Hills Golf and Country Club in Orlando, honoring blind golfers. *Gordon told the story about Arnie, being a nice guy, offered to play a round of golf with the champion blind golfer. The blind golfer accepted on the condition that they make a bet. Being a sportsman, Arnie agreed,* *suggesting a $10 Nassau (a $10 bet on the front nine, a $10 bet on the back nine and a $10 bet on the eighteen). The blind golfer said, "I'm thinking of a $1,000. Nassau". Arnie fidgeted, trying to think of an inoffensive way to get out of it, but the blind golfer insisted so Arnie finally gave in. "O.K,", Arnie agreed, "when shall we start?". The blind golfer answered, "Tonight at midnight".*

※

In addition to turning many casual drinkers into drunks, free liquor spawned another unheard of phenomenon: it made Gus the Bartender a very rich man. Instead of leaving a dollar or two tip at the bar, it was not uncommon for the habitual patrons to leave a five, a ten or even a twenty.

※

The golf course was a challenging championship layout. Early on, the club sponsored pro-am outings (a tour professional is teamed with three home course amateurs) that attracted many professional tour players on their off-days. I remember when I was teamed up with Leonard Thompson, who had just come off winning the record shattering prize money of $50,000 at the (long defunct) PGA tour stop, the Jackie Gleason Classic at the Country Club of Miami.

✤

Our Men's Club, of which I was the default chairman,[1] had joined with four other golf clubs in the area for "home and away" inter club golf matches. Playing "away" on different courses and making new friends was good sport, and, of course, our women golfers had their own inter club matches. The chairwoman of our Ladies' Club asked me what I thought of playing a men's and ladies' inter course match at our club on the same day.

✤

J eane had no interest in golf. As a member of Kansas City's Oakwood Country Club, where her dad and brothers golfed, she had taken some lessons from the pro, Bunny Torpey, but never followed through. She surprised me one day by asking if she took tennis lessons, could we have some togetherness playing tennis. I thought it was an excellent idea. Jeane signed up with Mary, the assistant pro, for ten lessons. At the completion of the lessons, I asked if she was ready to play. "No" she hesitatingly replied, "What happened was Mary gave me lessons playing right handed. I think I could do much better playing left handed". Jeane signed up for ten left handed lessons with Marty, the head pro. At the completion of the lessons, she said she was

---

[1] No one else would take the job.

ready. I lobbed the ball to her, but the ball passed by her and hit the back fence before she started to swing at it. "Don't hit it so hard", she complained. "I have no depth perception". A few more lobs ended our togetherness on the tennis courts. It was not a complete loss, however, she did look great in many of her new tennis outfits.

Jeane planned my fiftieth birthday party at the Sky Lake Country Club. Marian and Jerome flew in for the occasion. The club had golf apartments attached to the clubhouse which guests of members could rent for $35.00 a night, free golf fees included. Jerome, renowned for his capacity to devour scotch whiskey, combined with his love of golf, truly believed that he had died and gone to heaven: a week of unlimited scotch whiskey, unlimited golf and luxury accommodations for a mere $35.00 a night! [1]

---

[1] See Notes, Chapter 16, "Jerome Grossman"

My 50thwith Jerome and Midge

84

Chapter 17
THE ART OF TIPPING

Before the Sky Lake Country Club was built, our social and my golf life was centered around the nearby Presidential Golf and Country Club, a semi-private club with a famous Steak House open to the public. I golfed and had lunch there several times a week. Jeane and I were frequent patrons for dinner at the Steak House. Because there was often a waiting time at lunch and dinner before being seated, I habitually slipped Raphael, the maître d`, a two dollar tip at lunch and a five at dinner, even if the place was empty. Some friends thought I was nuts, but I assured them it would pay off when I needed him. That habit went on for almost two years. Fast forward to the Sky Lake Country Club.

The Fuchs, Shapiros, Gelmans and Oppenheims had a dinner date at the Sky Lake Country Club on a Saturday night at the height of the season. Around 6:00 that evening we received calls from the food director that because of an electrical problem in the kitchen, our 7:30 dinner reservation had been cancelled. "Not to worry", I assured our dinner companions, "my friend Raphael at the Presidential Steak House will take care of us". I called Raphael, gave him my name, and explained the emergency nature of my late request for a reservation. "Sorry, Mr. Opium", he apologized, "we are completely booked up for the night". Not discouraged, even though my name didn't ring a bell, I felt certain that once we were there he would recognize me and take care of us. The Steak House was packed. When I shook Raphael's hand I slipped him a twenty (five dollars for each of us) in his palm. "No problem", he said. We waited while others around us were being seated. Actually, there was a problem. It was getting late. I asked Raphael if he remembered that I gave him a twenty dollar bill. He remembered. I asked him to return it, which he did, and we left.

Chapter 18
THE P7 RPLE RAINCOAT
1971

Joye Tatz, Jeane's longtime friend, living in Los Angeles, called to ask if she would accompany her on a six week trip to Europe. Jeane enthusiastically accepted. When Joye sent her the itinerary of when and where they would visit, Jeane methodically put together what she would wear. The one thing she was lacking, and couldn't find, was a zip-in, zip-out raincoat. At dinner one evening with our friends, Eugene and Angie Lerner, Eugene thought he could take care of the problem. Eugene was the South Florida supervisor of Lerner's nationwide chain of ladies ready-to-wear stores. Eugene came through with a zip-in, zip-out purple raincoat. Her travel wardrobe completed, Jeane left to meet Joye in New York, where they would fly to London together.

My first letter from Jeane was a beautifully hand written seven page travelogue of the museums, art galleries, castles and churches that they had already visited. She loved everything, except as noted in the P.S. to the letter, **"I can't stand my purple raincoat."** The letters that followed were more of the same, with the addition of her purchase of a new zip-in, zip-out raincoat in Paris, and their visits to the vineyards in France, the casinos and mansions in Monte Carlo, the villas and historical sites in Italy, the Opera House and Palaces in Vienna and the castles in Spain. I thought they had seen it all, but they repeated the trip the following year. On the second trip, however, there was less time spent in cultural pursuits and more time spent in shopping with British pounds, French and Swiss francs and Italian lira.

Which reminds me of a joke about two school chums who met accidentally three years after graduation. They had lunch and brought each other up to date. Here is a transcript of their conversation:
FIRST LADY: I really lucked out. I married a man of means and we travel a lot. Last year in London my husband bought me a stunning 10 carat flawless diamond from Graff Jewelers.
SECOND LADY: That's fantastic.
FIRST LADY: From there we went to Paris where we visited the Louvre and my husband was able to negotiate a deal to buy me an original Rembrandt.
SECOND LADY: That's fantastic.
FIRST LADY: You must remember how I loved sports cars. In Italy my husband surprised me with a special edition Lamborghini that will shipped here next month.
SECOND LADY: That's fantastic.

FIRST LADY: *So what have you been doing?*
SECOND LADY: *I decided to go to finishing school.*
FIRST LADY: *A finishing school? What do they teach you at finishing school?*
SECOND LADY: *One thing they taught me was to say "fantastic" instead of " bullshit".*

Of course I missed Jeane a lot during her trips abroad, but, dear reader, let me explain why I am not going to emote about it. While we were living in Wichita, my business entailed a lot of traveling. I had the guilts about leaving Jeane on her own to take care of the kids and all household and business matters while I was away. She couldn't have been happy about it, but she never complained. My point is this: turnabout is fair play. After all she went through back then, she deserved to get away and to be able to enjoy the freedom of doing something she had always dreamed about doing. If that's not loving her, then God never made little green apples.

Madrid, 1971
The new raincoat

Chapter 19
LIL AND LOUIS

At the age of 31, in 1950, Louis was diagnosed with lymphoma. Living in Ann Arbor and being treated with the advanced technology available at the University of Michigan, the cancer went into remission. Five years later, unfortunately, it reappeared, and his remaining years until he passed away at age 56 were in-again, out-again hospital stays. He lived his out-again years to the fullest. To escape the Michigan winters he and Marilyn moved to Palm Aire. Before moving he had built the Marilyn Shop into a mini chain of five stores in the Detroit suburbs.

Throughout his Ann Arbor days, Marilyn's mother, Lil, was active in the business. Lil retired and lived in Miami Beach several years before Louis and Marilyn made the move. It seems that while working in the stores up North, Lil and Lou got along best when ignoring each other. Louis once told me that Nixon had mismanaged the war in Vietnam because all he had to do was send Lil over there and she would have gotten that mess straightened out real fast.

Then there was the incident when Lil called Marilyn and she got their answering machine with the message, "This is Louis Oppenheim. Thank you for calling. We are unable to speak with you at this time, but if you will kindly leave your name and number and we will return your call as soon as possible". When Marilyn called back the following day, Lil told her she had called yesterday and had a nice conversation with Louis.

Of course there are two sides to every story. While still living in Ann Arbor, Louis's and Marilyn's daughters, Jill and Cathy, as youngsters, during school vacations, visited their grandmother Lil in Miami Beach. As Cathy recently related to me, during a visit when she was ten years old, her behavior had apparently annoyed her grandmother. Finally, her grandmother figure-ed out Cathy's problem: She was too much like her father.

Golf was Louis's life. After he moved to Palm Aire he was part of an Iowa foursome that included Les Bookey from Des Moines, Paul Siegel from Davenport and Jordan Ginsberg from Sioux City. Outside of his close circle of friends, Jordan adopted the name Jay Jordan, which he apparently thought was more acceptable in his extensive business dealings. He may have been a good business man, but he was a lousy golfer. Finally, the other three told Jordan he was out of the foursome until his game improved. Jordan signed up for golf lessons, using his business name, Jay Jordan. After his embarrassing first lesson he despondently said to the pro, "I guess I'm the worst golfer at Palm Aire", to which the pro replied, "I don't think so. I keep hearing terrible things about a Jordan Ginsberg".

Chapter 20
A CLASH OF CULTURES

Bill called to tell us he was going to be married to Connie, a classmate, at Wichita State University. The wedding ceremony was to be at Sausalito, California. I called my mother, Goldie, living in Des Moines and arranged for her to spend a few days with us in Las Vegas before heading to Sausalito. Mom had never been to Las Vegas, and had no interest in gambling, so she spent her time watching the compulsive players at the one armed bandit machines. When she heard the clinking and clanking of jackpot coins being ejected from the bandits, she would rush over to congratulate and interview the winners.

The wedding site at Sausalito, overlooking San Francisco Bay and the Golden Gate Bridge, was spectacular. The ceremony was secular. Bill was still a hippie. All of his friends who attended the wedding were hippies, fresh from Salvation Army stores, dressed for the occasion. The most interesting aspect of the wedding, however, was the culture clash. Connie's mother was Governor Ronald Reagan's press secretary. Enough said.

Chapter 21
JEANE & HAROLD OPPENHEIM
Designers & Manufacturers of Fine Jewelry

While operating Oppenheim Distributors, Jeane and I had been involved in manufacturing some of the jewelry items we sold, thus we had experience in jewelry design and manufacturing before opening our own business. Jeane, who was a student of fashion design at the Kansas City Art Institute, now delved into jewelry design. Our sample lines were a mixture of some of her original designs and also designs available at commercial casting companies.

ORIGINAL DESIGNS BY JEANE

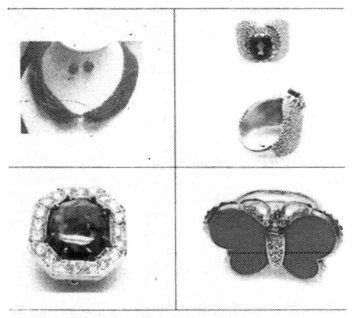

UPPER LEFT: 16" choker made of 6 twisted strands of oxblood coral beads and 14 karat gold polished beads. 14 karat gold clasp.

UPPER RIGHT: 18 karat gold ring, upswept styling, hobnail finish, set with a cushion shape tanzanite surrounded with diamonds.

LOWER LEFT: 14 KARAT GOLD PENDANT centering a Gilson created black opal accented with diamonds.

LOWER RIGHT: 14 karat gold butterfly ring set with salmon color coral wings accented with diamonds.

Not wishing to get involved with credit problems, we sold only to jewelers with top credit ratings. To keep our local sales rep happy, we made an exception by selling to a friend of his, Ronnie, who was opening a new store in Hollywood (Florida). To instill my confidence, Ronnie showed me a bank deposit receipt of $50,000. That was impressive, but when I visited his store before he opened, I figured more than half of that was already spent on fixtures, and there was no telling how much of a salary he had already drawn. We shipped Ronnie an opening order of $7,500, payable in five monthly installments of $1,500. The first two installments went unpaid. There was nothing to gain by suing him or turning it over to a bill collector, so I just kept in touch, hoping that our friendship would someday pay off. It did. Ronnie called one day to tell me he had good news: his store was robbed. He paid us in full when he received his insurance settlement. All's well that ends well.

Jeane developed a private business that flourished, selling to her friends, and to friends of her friends, ad infinitum. Her sale proceeds were deposited in her own piggy bank. I concluded that Jeane was a merchandoing genius. Think about it: in her private business ran out of the company's office[1], she had no cost of the goods sold and no overhead expense. She made 100% profit on every sale. As occasionally happens, a jewelry item had to be returned because a stone came loose from its setting, or it was otherwise in need of repair. She was sorry about the inconvenience to her customer, and escorted her to the repair department, my office.

---

[1] I use the word "office" loosely. Actually, she was a walking showroom, selling rings and things that she was wearing.

Chapter 22
PALM SPRINGS

Come the first week in February, Jeane and I would make our annual pilgrimage to Tucson to attend the world's premier Gem and Mineral Show. Hundreds of exhibitors from around the world set up displays at about fifty locations throughout the city, most of them open to the public, others requiring bona fide dealer verification to gain entry. It was an unparalleled showcase for everything new in jewelry styling and was the premier marketplace for buying unusual gemstones.

From Tucson, en route home, we sometimes visited my sister Eskie in Palm Springs. Eskie is seven years younger than I but despite that at this writing she is eighty three and has nine great-grandchildren, I still think of her as my kid sister. My memory goes back to when Eskie was eight years old, living in Des Moines, where the winter ice often formed a skating rink in our backyard for the neighborhood kids. On a night when our parents and older sisters were out, when Louis and I were hosting a poker game for our high school slackers, a knock was heard on our back door. I investigated the knock, to be told by a neighborhood kid that Eskie was crying. I returned to the game and reported the unimportant news to the indifferent poker players, explaining that Eskie was crying, but Eskie cries a lot. Later, when Nettie and Dorothy returned home, I informed them that Eskie was in the backyard, crying. They found her lying on the ice with a fractured leg.

Eskie once explained to me the difference between a mother and a mother-in-law. Eskie, then a mother of three pre-teenagers, Wendy, Arny and Joe, was complaining to her mother-in-law, Becky, that taking care of the outrageous demands of the kids and the household chores were wearing her out. Becky's advice was, "Eskie, honey, it would be better if you cut back on your running around and card playing, and devote more quality time to understanding your children's needs". Later that day, Eskie phoned the same complaint to her mother, Goldie. Goldie's advice was, "Eskie, honey, it's time for you to take a vacation away from the kids and have the maid come in more often".

If the producers of American Idol ran a great grandmother division, Eskie would easily win.

She's so pretty, she's so witty,

She can write and sing her own ditty.

Eskie and Mickey Engman bought a home in Palm Springs, but before they moved in, Mickey, at age 63, passed away. Years later, Eskie married another Mickey, Mickey Shepard. The second time around for both Eskie and Mickey has worked out just great. A plus for Eskie in duplicating her spouse's first name the second time around is that it eliminates the worry about Freudian slips – besides not having to change the monogram on her towels.

Chapter 23
TOO JEWISH

When we started to manufacture jewelry in 1974 the International Gold Market hovered around $175 an ounce. In 1980 the market had climbed to $850 an ounce. Our sales plummeted as rapidly as the gold prices soared. We decided to call it quits and close out our inventory to jewelers at bargain prices. One of the buyers was Vernon Jewelers in the Coastal Shopping Mall in Naples. To consummate the deal, we offered to assist them with a "Special Purchase" Sale to enable them to recoup part of their investment. Vernon Jewelers' ad copy read, "We have acquired the diamond and fine jewelry inventory of Jeane and Harold Oppenheim, designers and manufacturers of fine jewelry ......blah...blah...blah".

Back then, Naples (Florida) was a city of about 20,000 permanent residents that octupled in season as a tourist destination for the rich and famous, most of whom were WASPS, (White Anglo Saxon Protestants). The permanent Jewish population and their seasonal influx were zilch. Allow me, dear reader, to take you on a magic carpet ride back to Wichita and introduce you to Irv and Estelle Priceman. Irv and I played golf and sat in our bi-weekly poker games together. Estelle was a well liked, very pleasant lady, but there was something about her, -- and I say this with no disparaging intent, as a matter of fact, it could be a compliment – that, to me, was the essence of Jewishness. Was it a composite of the way she dressed?...her hair-do?...her gestures?...her smile?... Her mannerisms?.... I don't know.

The Pricemans, retired and living in Naples, had read Vernon Jewelers ad and, to our surprise, stopped in the store to see us. Jeane and I met them for dinner that night and reminisced about old times. To me, Estelle living in Naples was like a fish out of water, a Jew in the Waspian Sea. "How long have you been here?", I asked. "Five years", she replied. I followed up with, "So, what do you think of Naples?" Estelle, smiling (that Jewish smile?), thought for awhile, and then sighed, "It's o.k., but it's getting too Jewish".

Jeane retired after we closed our jewelry manufacturing business. At the ripe old age of 62, I enrolled in the Gemological Institute of America's (GIA) study courses with the goal of becoming a professional jewelry appraiser by combining my extensive marketing experience with comprehensive gemological knowledge. After acquiring GIA's Graduate

Gemologist (GG) diploma, I joined the American Society of Appraisers (ASA) and earned their coveted Master Gemologist / Appraiser (MGA) certification, launching my new career as a professional jewelry appraiser. (More on that later).

Chapter 24
THE DOUBLE WHAMMY

We never asked how or when his first marriage ended, but years later, while in graduate school back at Wichita State University, Bill married a classmate, Sharon, and legally adopted her two young sons, Mike and Richie, from a previous marriage. Bill was finishing a Masters' in English, but was obsessed with thoroughbred horse breeding and racing. In response to his resume` sent worldwide, he was offered a journalist's job at Hoofbeats, a New Zealand racing and breeding publication. Bill and his new family spent about two years in New Zealand before Bill felt that he had gone about as far as he could go, and Sharon, a highly educated women's libber, found the New Zealander's syndrome of "keep 'em pregnant and in the kitchen" to be about a century behind times.

Upon their return to the States, they took interim jobs in Covington, Louisiana before heading for the big league of thoroughbred breeding, Lexington, Kentucky. Bill wrote and published a newsletter for the racing and breeding industry and became a consultant to breeders. Sharon extended her education and became a psychologist, focusing

107

on helping battered women. Their diverse interests and orientations, however, ultimately led to a divorce.

✤

The divorce proceedings were a double whammy for Bil. To promote big time thoroughbred breeding and the racing industry, Oaklawn Park Race Track, in Hot Springs, Arkansas, put up a million dollar bonus for any horse that could win the Rebel Stakes and the Arkansas Derby at Oaklawn, and go on to win the Kentucky Derby a month later. Bil's first big consulting client, third-generation timberman John Ed Anthony, of Fordyce, Arkansas, had bred, on Bil's recommendation, and now owned a colt called Demons Begone, who had won the two Arkansas races and went off hot favorite for the 198U Kentucky Derby. Unfortunately he bled after a furlong and was pulled up.

Chapter 25
MIKE AND RICHIE

Beginning at their approximate ages of eight and five, respectively, our windfall grandsons, Mike and Richie, were our house guests for several weeks every summer. The four of us vacationed at tourist destinations in South and Central Florida: Disney World, the Colony Resort and Tennis Club at Longboat Key (Sarasota), several spots in the Florida Keys from Key Largo to Key West, and the West Coast from Marco Island to Sanibel Island. After running out of places to go, we bought a two-week timeshare condominium on Fort Myers Beach. Most days were spent poolside, deep sea fishing or gathering sea shells. To satisfy the appetites of growing boys, we patronized buffet dinners a lot. When the young sophisticates were treated to an occasional gourmet dinner, Mike's favorite was beef Wellington and Richie's choice was any fancy shrimp dish on the menu. Memorable moments, like the one when I noticed that our car's odometer turned exactly 50,000 miles, were commemorated with Richie's toast "Let's break out the cookies". They were fun, carefree days and nights that lasted until the boys found other interests in life, like girls.

Without Mike and Richie, we lost interest in the time share condo and offered it our sons, Bill and Jim. Jim and Robin, who spent their summer vacations at Cape Cod with Robin's parents had no interest in the timeshare. Bill and his wife, Lou, accepted the gift but never stayed in the Fort Meyers Beach timeshare. They did, however, trade it once. The bottom line was that neither Bill nor Lou could stand the paperwork involved so they foisted the timeshare on to the younger generation, Mike and Richie. Not surprisingly, Mike and Richie coped with the paperwork and have gotten genuine pleasure from the gift. Thus, for them, the timeshare condominium went full circle from being guests of their grandparents as kids to owners as adults. We always stayed in touch with Mike, a professional photographer married to Muriel, and her son Cole from her previous marriage, living in Asheville, and with Richie, who works for the State of California, living with his partner, Bernard, in Los Angeles.

110

At Longboat Key, Sarasota

Chapter 26
THE MATCHMAKER

During her growing up years in Kansas City, Marilyn Baker was almost a part of the Navran family. Marilyn dated Jeane's brother Bob, then Brother Dick, then brother Roger, but she forsook all three and married John Weil. Jeane and Marilyn renewed their friendship when the Weil's moved to Coral Gables. *Hardly anyone is still around to remember the radio days of Don Ameche and Francis Langford as the Bickermans. It was a weekly half hour radio program of throwing barbs at each other.* As entertainment, listening to the bickering was fun, but in real life, spending evenings with the reincarnated Bickermans, Marilyn and John, as Jeane and I often did, was very uncomfortable. Their barb throwing marriage ended in a hostile divorce.

Meanwhile, with an ulterior motive, of course, Jeane frequently called our widower friend, Teddy Blake, to ask, "what good is sitting alone every night?". He tired of the calls and agreed to have dinner with us and a friend. Thus, Teddy met Marilyn. After dinner Marilyn invited us to her apartment for coffee and dessert. When a respectable time had elapsed, I said, "O.K., Teddy, it's time to go". Teddy quickly replied,

"I'm not going anyplace". Soon thereafter, Teddy and Marilyn were married. I know many of my dear readers are poetry lovers, so I will share with you my toast to the newlyweds:

When her marriage to John came undone
Mir* kept her well known aplomb
Instead of the strife
She found a new life
Filled with romance and laughter and fun

For she met a nice man, known as Teddy
Who knew not that he was ready
To find love anew
But it suddenly grew
And without Viagra, holds steady

*Mir is the nickname given to Marilyn by her grandchildren.

Marilyn, for years, had been active in the Women's Auxiliary at the Miami Home for the Aged. After their marriage, Teddy also got involved. He was (and at age 91, still is) an avid golfer. Teddy organized a game of wheelchair golf, thus, to my knowledge, became the first golf professional at any home for the aged.

Chapter 27
WEDDING BELLS
FOR JIM AND ROBIN
1983

Instead of flying to Cape Cod to attend our son Jim's wedding, we decided to take a driving tour to visit some historic landmarks in the Northeast along the way. We spent a night and next day in Williamsburg soaking up colonial history; then two days in Washington, where our main attractions were the Hall of Gems and Minerals at the Smithsonian, Mount Vernon, the pandas at the zoo, and Mrs. Simpson's Tea House (Jeane went gaga over everything British, possibly because of her mother's English roots). Our next stop was Niagara Falls, where other than observing the breathtaking ferocity of the falls, our interest focused on the George Bernard Shaw Festival at Niagara-on-the-Lake, Canada (more of jolly old England).

Son Jim and Robin Reeves were married at Robin's grandfather's estate in North Truro, Cape Cod, Massachusetts. Both Jim and Robin were disciples of Avatar Meher Baba. Robin and Jim had become romantically involved the year before although they had known each other casually for a few years. Jeane and I never made an attempt to understand the

Avatar's teachings, but they played an important part in making Jim and Robin the kind, considerate, loving people they are, and that was good enough for us. Following their honeymoon they returned to Columbia, South Carolina to start a family and where Dr. Jim resumed his chiropractic practice and Robin her career as a licensed clinical social worker.

Growing up, their family spent summer vacations at Cape Cod, thus we didn't have the opportunity to spend as much time with Jim's kids as we did with Bill's. We did, however, enjoy Josh as our house guest when we enrolled him in a month long golf clinic at our club, but when we invited Jon the following summer, he declined. Jon was too busy tinkering with cars.

At this writing their son Josh, twenty five, is preparing for an extended stay to India, who, like Larry in Somerset Maugham's excellent novel and movie, "The Razor's Edge", went in search of spiritual learning and guidance to find his meaningful niche in life. As you read this, he is possibly already in India. Jon, twenty three, takes cars apart and puts them back together again. He is a student at a Georgia technical college and a parking valet at a posh Atlanta restaurant. His hobby is "drifting", the sport (?) of driving at a high speed then turning sharply and braking to see how far the car will skid. Under their back porch, there are several piles of burnt out tires that attest to his drifting hobby. Andrew, nineteen, is a drama student at Marymount College, New York City, and loves it. Christopher, ten, was adopted when he was two years old because his birth mother, Robin's half-sister, was unable to care for him.

En route home from Jim's and Robin's wedding, we toured the gilded age mansions of Newport. It was an interesting day, highlighted by a visit to the Astor mansion. We were greeted curbside by a valet who took our names and escorted us to the doorman. "Welcome, Mr. and Mrs. Oppenheim", the doorman spoke as he bowed, "Mrs. Astor will be so disappointed that she missed you, but she will be unable to be here today". It turned out that a troupe of actors and actresses in period dress were tour guides who escorted us through every nook and cranny of the home as it was originally furnished, replete with costumed guests who whispered to us intimate gossips about life in the gilded age, and the maid who served us tea and crumpets in the drawing room. It was a laugh-out-loud two hour fun tour.

Jim and Robin cutting the wedding cake, 1983

Josh (in center), the Bar Mitzvah boy, with
parents and brothers Andrew (left) and Jon

Chapter 28
THE LIFE AND TIMES OF A JEWELRY APPRAISER

Jewelry appraisals serve as both a customer amenity and a source of income for jewelry stores. Many full service jewelry stores have their own appraisal department. There were, however, many other jewelry stores that, for various reasons, outsourced appraisals to independent appraisers like myself. The outsourced procedure was that a client jewelry store would make appointments with their customers to bring in their jewelry at a designated time when I would be on premises to appraise their jewelry while they watched. The key words were, "while they watched". Customers loved the face-to-face appraisal sessions because, [1] they didn't have to leave their jewelry at the store, and [2] they liked learning more details about the characteristics of their jewelry items, and in some cases, historical backgrounds.

URam Jewelers was one of my jewelry store clients. One day in 1984, the administrator of the South Florida branch of the Drug Enforcement Administration (DEA) stopped in Uram's to ask if they had a jewelry appraiser. Congress had just enacted a law creating the Department of

Justice's Assets Forfeture Program. The program authorized seizure of criminals' assets, the proceeds of which were (and still are) subsequently used to further law enforcement activities. The law provides that the seized property must be first appraised and then funneled through the U.S. Marshal's office for disposition at approved auctions in the private sector. I happened to be in the right place at the right time. From that day in 1984 until I retired at the age of 87 in 2006, I was a contract jewelry appraiser for not only the South Florida DEA office, but also for the FBI, the FDA (Criminal Investigation Division), and the U.S. Attorney's Office.

NEW

As I write this, April 16, 2009, President Obama has lifted the travel and remittance embargo for U.S. citizens with family in Cuba. It reminded me of an interesting jewelry appraisal.

The Cuban exiles living in Florida were a monolithic group that wielded political clout far in excess of their numbers. For over a half century their implacable hatred of Castro has bullied our administrations – Democratic and Republican alike -- into enforcing an economic embargo that has done nothing to diminish Castro's grip on power, but has perpetuated the poverty of its inhabitants. Among other restrictions, the embargo limited to a pittance the amount of money that could be sent to family members living in Cuba. Thus, it came as a shock to me to learn of a lady living in Cuba who was able to financially help her relatives living in Miami. Here's the story.

I received a phone call from a gentleman who identified himself only as Jose, who had some jewelry that he wanted appraised stored in a safety deposit box. We arranged to meet at his bank. At the bank, I met not only with Jose, but with six of his relatives. We sat at a table in a secured conference room. Jose opened two large safety deposit boxes and emptied their contents on the table. After a fast scan I told them it was costume jewelry and they didn't need my services. "Not so fast", cautioned Jose, "please go over it piece by piece and separate the real from the fake". It seems that the assembled relatives had an aunt then living in Cuba who, over the years, was able to make several visits to Miami. On each visit she cleverly embedded some real jewelry in with an enormous amount of the junk jewelry she wore. The appraisal process separated 42 real rings and things that had an appraised current replacement value of close to a half million dollars.

Another unusual need for jewelry appraisal reports came my way via a phone call from Juan in San Juan, Puerto Rico. I had been recommended to him to appraise his inventory, and if I was interested, he would pay my expenses, including round trip airfare, to inspect his inventory and discuss his need. It was an offer I couldn't refuse. Juan was the distributor of Seiko watches for all of the Caribbean Islands. At that time Seiko was so popular it was like having a license to steal. Juan's business had grown to where he needed more space. The building that most suited his needs housed a ground floor jewelry store, owned by the building's owner. The owner would sell to Juan only if he agreed to buy the jewelry store and the building as a packaged deal. Juan bought both. The jewelry store did well. Juan opened a second store in the Las Americas mall in San Juan, the busiest shopping mall I had ever been in, and it was doing well. Juan aspired to open six new jewelry stores on the Islands. When Juan went to his bank for financing, he offered his inventory as part of his loan collateral. His banker looked over the inventory and said to Juan, "We're bankers, not jewelers. Come back to us with a jewelry appraisal from an independent appraiser with verifiable credentials".

Here, dear reader, if you're still with me, is where I came in. Juan and I made a deal. I estimated it would take four weeks to complete the appraisal, but the only way I could do it was to alternate one week in San Juan with two weeks at home, and that it would be all expenses paid, including lodging at the Carib Hilton for Jeane and me, plus our round trip airfares. Juan, surprisingly, agreed. There were perks that Juan voluntarily threw in, like having us chauffeur driven to and from his private club for dinners on his tab. Jeane loved it. She said she felt like Eloise, the legendary rich kid, the subject of the best selling children's book, "Eloise at the Plaza".

Everything went pretty much on schedule, except one morning when returning to San Juan, the captain announced that we were making an emergency landing at the Turks and Caicos Islands, midway between Miami and San Juan. After landing, we learned that there had been a bomb scare. All passengers were transported to a filthy shanty at the airport where the only food, greasy hamburgers and fried chicken, soon ran out, and the toilets overflowed. No member of the flight crew was ever sighted in the shanty. We later learned that they had spent the day mingling with the affluent vacationers at the Island's Club Med. A relief plane finally arrived eight hours later to take us to San Juan. The following morning the San Juan Star's front page headline read,

EASTERN AIRLINE FLIGHT TO SAN JUAN INTERRUPTED BY BOMB SCARE
Passengers and crew enjoyed a free vacation day at the Turks and Caicos' Club Med.

That added insult to injury. I ripped off a nasty letter to the Star explaining that the Eastern Airline's press release that they published was pure, unadulterated crap. I sent a copy of the letter to the Miami Herald. Neither of my letters was published, but it provided the spark that ignited my letters-to-the-editor writing. It probably isn't cricket to interject an advertisement for my first book, "My Letters-to-the-Editor That Never Got Published", a compilation of my opinions of George W. Bush during the 2004 presidential election campaign, but it's available at trafford.com/05-1518.

My Letters-to-the-Editor That Never Got Published

I think we got bushwacked

A Critique of
Our Immoral War President's

◇ Unnecessary war of choice against Iraq.
◇ Economic war against the middle class.
◇ Unconscionable war against the environment.
◇ War against our constitutional right of privacy.
◇ War to blur the separation of church and state.

A Compilation of Letters Written by
Harold Oppenheim
During Bush's despicable War for Re-election

To digress, when my niece, Jean Zeldin, heard that her aunt Jeane and uncle Harold were moving to Kansas City she called to tell us how pleased she was, and asked if I would do her a favor. Jean is the Executive Director of the Midwest Center for Holocaust Education, and among her many achievements, she has developed excellent rapport with the Kansas City Star. Jean had read my book, "My Letters to the Editor That Never Got Published". She said that she had no problem with my compulsive letter writing, which she felt certain would continue unabated after I moved to Kansas City. *The favor she asked of me, however, was that I would promise never to let the Kansas City Star know that she and I were related.*

Juan's jewelry store was one of the approved places provided by cruise ship directors to passengers who disembarked to shop in San Juan while their ship was in port. I kid you not, every time a ship was in port, a line of buyers formed to get in Juan's store. I am going back over twenty five years, and things may have changed, but back then a cruise director's life was idyllic, -- the luxurious life aboard ship, plus the shakedown of merchants at each port –of-call. I witnessed Juan's store manager hand the cruise director an envelope of $200.00 cash as payment to qualify for listing on the cruise directors' approved places to shop. Think about it: If there were only ten approved places to shop at each port-of-call, multiply $200.00 times the number of ports-of-call, times the number of stops per year at each port, all undeclared, tax free cash income, and you'll understand why, if reincarnated, I would choose to come back as a cruise director.

Chapter 29
CRUISING AND ISLAND HOPPING

A *generation ago, when popular music had melodies and the lyrics made sense, Steve Lawrence and his wife Edie Gorme` were top concert performers. Between songs, Steve amused the audience with banter, mostly about Edie. It seems that Edie was complaining to Steve that she was exhausted and wanted to get away and relax; in particular, to a place she had never been. Steve suggested that she try the kitchen.*

Two things Jeane had in common with Edie: They loved to get away and relax and they had an aversion to the kitchen. We took ;request ;un-;illed Caribbean cruises on the big ships. The routine was pretty much the same: dress ;or break;ast; break;ast; change to sun bathing attire; lounge on a sun deck; mid-morning snacks; shower; dress ;or lunch; lunch; nap; dress ;or a;ternoon activities, a shore trip or stay aboard ;or the choice o; a guest speaker, dance lessons, bingo, movie, reading, cards, casino (some ships), shopping; tea and biscuits; dressy change (jackets) ;or dinner; drinks and snacks at the bar; dinner; show time; late night pizza snacks; bedtime. That's six meals a day counting snacks, but who's counting?

❧

The Windjammer "tall sailing ship" cruises we took, as the name, implies, were more adventuresome, and because the harbors were too shallow (at that time) for the big ships, the ports-of-call were less commercial. After our first few big ship cruises we rarely went ashore for sightseeing and shopping, but on the Windjammer cruises we didn't miss a chance to go ashore on the unspoiled, friendlier islands of Antigua, St. Kitts, St. Barts (French, with topless sun bathers), Nevis and Martinique, all of the ports with interesting sightseeing and most with at least one first class restaurant.

❧

We booked passage on a Mackay Airlines flight from Fort Lauderdale to Eleuthera, an outer Bahamas Island that is a hundred and ten mile long strip of white sand beaches strewn with gigantic pink seashells. We spent a week there as beach bums. Mackay Airlines was a fleet of small island hopping planes, carrying up to thirty two passengers. When boarding the plane for the return flight to Fort Lauderdale, the lady boarding in front of me turned and whispered, "Where do they keep the parachutes?" She apparently knew more than I did because while in flight over the ocean the captain announced that he didn't have enough fuel to get back to Fort Lauderdale. *It reminded me of the Lufthansa story that* goes, *"when the plane had run out of fuel and was gliding down toward the ocean, the captain's instructions were, 'the passengers who can swim get on the right wing, the passengers who can't swim get on the left wing, and thank you for flying Lufthansa'"*. Our plight wasn't that drastic. We had enough fuel to make it to the shitty airport at Bimini, but at least we were on dry land, where we waited six hours before being flown back to Fort Lauderdale.

Chapter 30
THE SOUTHERN HEBREW
INVITATIONAL TOURNAMENT

The Southern Hebrew Invitational Tournament was a three weekend getaway golf and social event one summer, played by eight S.H.I.T. golfers at Naples, West Palm Beach and Boca Raton golf courses, and a championship tour stop for their wives' shopping. Prizes were awarded each night at dinner, to the day's lowest net scoring golfer and, at an afternoon's show-and-tell event, to the shopper who saved the most money that day on her purchases. The grand prize, awarded at the last night's dinner was to go to the person who told the funniest golf joke. The three finalists were:

1 The wife of a golfer went to the pro shop to buy a gift for her husband, explaining to the pro that she and her husband had a terrible fight last night and she wanted to buy him something to make him feel better.
PRO: Here is a putter your husband had been eyeing that would certainly make him happy.
WIFE: Done. Have it engraved "From your loving wife".
PRO: That's not a good idea. When his buddies read that they will never stop kidding him.

WIFE: *What do you suggest?*

PRO: *Engrave something that will help his putting, like "Never up, never in".*

WIFE: *No way. That's what our fight was about.*

2 *A newcomer super senior (really old) single golfer, looking for a game, asked the starter to be paired with someone with good eyesight because he would need help finding his ball. The starter paired him with another super senior who assured the newcomer that he had good vision. The newcomer teed off:*

NEWCOMER: *Did you see where my ball went?*

PARTNER: *Yes, I saw it.*

NEWCOMER: *Where did it go?*

PARTNER: *I can't remember.*

3 *A couple riding in their golf cart:*

SHE: *If I go first, would you remarry?*

HE: *Forget it, let's think golf.*

SHE: *No, think about this: If I go first, would you remarry?*

HE: *I don't know. I've never thought about it.*

SHE: *Think about it. If I go first, would you remarry?*

HE: *Alright, enough already.*

SHE: *If you did remarry, would you give her my five carat diamond ring?*

HE (Thinking about it): *I don't know, but you know how jewelers are, I'd get only a fraction of what it's worth when I'd go to sell it.*

SHE: *Is that a yes or a no?*

HE: *It's a maybe.*
SHE: *What about my Mercedes convertible?*
HE: *Why would I need two cars?*
SHE: *Is that a yes or a no?*
HE: *It's a maybe.*
SHE: *Would you give her my set of Calloway golf clubs?*
HE: *Not a chance. She's left handed.*

You pick the winner[1].

---

[1] It was number 3.

Chapter 31
MRS. WILLIAM J. OPPENHEIM, IV
Bill's Fourth Marriage
1995

Many alert readers must have noticed that I skipped Bill's third marriage, to Michal. She was a lovely lady, and my only reason for omitting her is that their marriage was short lived and, in my unsolicited opinion, a rebound.

Jeane and I were visiting Bill in Lexington at the same time that Louise Radford (the lady known as Lou), a Brit, was visiting her friend Roger, a friend and also an associate of Bill's. Lou and Roger had met when they were both teaching English in Turkey and later kept in touch. Jeane spent a lot of time with Lou and loved her wit and wisdom. Being a Brit was the frosting. As a journalist and consultant to thoroughbred horse breeders, Bill made frequent trips to Newmarket, near London. As Lou later explained it to me, "We really WERE 'just friends' – until one time he visited, as he always did, on the way to Newmarket sales, and, as I always put it, it was the same light, but the prism moved and I (we) saw different colors – we'd fallen in love. We never had an affair". After that "one" visit, upon his return to Lexington, Bill had to face a difficult decision, and he chose the honest one. He informed Michal that he had fallen in love and asked for a divorce. He agreed to the terms of the divorce that virtually separated him from his worldly possessions, but that's what love is all about.

❈

Lou's mother was widowed, so Bill wanted to ask her mother, Betty, ;or her daughter's hand in marriage. While at Betty's, Lou le;t Bill ;or what she thought would be a twenty minute con;erence with Betty (it lasted over an hour). Lou later told me that Betty con;ronted Bill with two ;orthright questions: (1) "Well, your track record isn't very good. What changed?" (2) "So, are you a compulsive gambler?" I don't know how Bill answered Betty's ;irst question; as regards the second question, he believes that ;or knowledgeable players like himsel;, betting on horses is sa;er than betting on the stock market.

When Bill noti;ied his parents o; his plans to marry Lou, Jeane's response was, "What took you so long? The minute I met her I could have told you it would happen". When Bill asked Jeane why she hadn't told him that years ago, her reply was "You wouldn't have listened". In 1995, Bill and Lou were married in Scotland, where they purchased a 140 year old, three story house in the Central Highlands, overlooking spectacular Loch Tay.

136

Wedding Day, May 13, 1995

L ou has a whimsical humor about Bill's previous marriages. During her first visit to North Miami Beach, Jeane was giving Lou the Cook's Tour of our condo, which had a long wall of family pictures. Lou stopped in front of the picture shown below, when Bill was six years old, dancing with his seven year old cousin Jean, the ring bearer and flower girl, respectively, at their uncle Bob's wedding.

"Your first marriage?" Lou asked Bill.

Lou's whimsical humor about Bil's previous marriages is as spontaneous as it is clever. The "IV" following "Mrs. William J. Oppenheim" in this chapter's heading is a double entendre. One obvious meaning is that the "IV" means "Bil's Fourth Marriage". But here's the story of the real meaning of "IV":

Bil and Lou attend the annual Royal Ascot, a major event in the British social calendar. The Royal enclosure has a strict dress code: male attendees must wear full morning dress, including a top hat; ladies must adhere to many restrictions and must wear hats. If you have seen the stage play or movie "My Fair Lady", you get the picture. Another "must" is the name badge: ladies are forbidden to use their given first name, thus "Mrs. Louise Oppenheim" is a no-no, & must be "Mrs. William J. Oppenheim". Not to be intimidated by the lineage of the aristocratic blood lines at Ascot, Lou simply appended the "IV" to her "Mrs. William J. Oppenheim" name badge.

William J. Oppenheim
Mrs. William J. Oppenheim, IV
In Ascot Regalia

Chapter 32
OUR GANG

What began as vacation getaways with Midge and Jerome evolved into including other long time ;riends, Bob and Babe Mallin (Kansas City), Sam and Jane Rankin (Albuquerque) and Bill and Joye Tatz, (Los Angeles). In subsequent summers some or all o; the couples met at Hilton Head, South Carolina; Escondida, Cali;ornia; Broome Park, near Dover, England; London; Pitlochry, Scotland; and Lake Tahoe/Napa Valley/San Francisco.

❧

While staying at a bed and break;ast in Pitlochry, we drove to get a starting time at the Royal and Ancient Gol; Course at St. Andrew's. The starter said the best he could do was to give us a starting time ;or the ;ollowing year. He also suggested that we may be able to get on at St. Andrew's new course. Never having heard that there was a new course at St. Andrews, it piqued my curiosity. "How old is the new course?" I asked. "102 years old", the starter replied.

❧

The ;irst stop on our planned trip to Lake Tahoe, Napa Valley and San Francisco, was Reno, where we would rent a car and drive to Lake Tahoe. Inasmuch as our wives, the Navran sisters, Jeane and Midge, were notoriously famous for the huge amount of luggage they traveled with, Jerome and I decided to rent separate cars. When Jeane and I arrived in Reno, the rental car agency's van met us at the airport to take us to the agency office where we would pick up our rental car. After the driver loaded Jeane's luggage on the van, I apologized for all the work it involved, to which he replied, "This is nothing, mister. You should have seen the luggage belonging to a lady who was here about an hour ago". The lady was sister Midge.

❀

We had dinner one evening at the Edgewood Golf Course, reputed to be Lake Tahoe's finest. After a round of drinks at the bar, we placed our dinner order. We waited and waited, and drank and drankf it seemed forever before the dinners arrived. When dinner was served, the orders were mixed up beyond recognition. Before we got too upset, however, the manager arrived to explain the problem. The American Celebrity Golf Classic, an annual event at Edgewood, just completed, left the kitchen staff so distraught that they all had quit. The manager explained that he was breaking in a new crew and apologized for the mish mash. The drinks and dinners were on the house.

At Lake Tahoe: left to right: Joye and Bill Tatz,
Midge and Jerome Grossman, Babe and Bob
Mallin, Jeane and Harold Oppenheim.

EPILOGUE

When Jim was a wee lad, Jeane and I discovered the most effective inducement to get him to bed was to read to him episodes of Charles Schultz's "Peanuts". Jim was entertained by the trials and tribulations of Charlie Brown, Lucy, Linus and the entire cast of characters. I learned some lessons of life from the episodes. One of my favorites was Charlie Brown's reply when Linus asked him how his birdhouse project was coming along. Charlie replied, *"I was sent the wrong set of plans. The lumberyard sold me green lumber that warped when it got wet. I bought the wrong size nails. All things considered, the birdhouse is coming along fine"*.

When my solicitous family, relatives and friends ask how I am getting along, my ready reply is, *"All things considered, I'm doing fine"*. As anyone who has lost a loved one knows, it's tough. I have no words of wisdom for the grief that, sooner or later, all mortals will share. In my case, writing this book has been therapeutic.

Taking the advice of the poet William Blake, who centuries ago wrote, "The busy bee has no time for sorrow", I have started on my next project, going through volumes of photograph albums to create a video. Like this book, the simple meaning of the plot will be to tell them that I loved her a lot.

Sneak Preview of my new video project

Canongate

Willie Trump and his sons (the 7outh African Trumps, not related to Donald Trump), developers of Williams Island residential community and resort, were owners of The Williams Island Golf and Country Clu8 (originally The 7ky Lake Golf and Country Clu8), with an estimated market value of $7 million dollars as a going 8usiness. Williams Island su8mitted a proposal to the county commissioners to rezone their 158 acre golf course for housing development. The rezoning proposal was fought 8y the area's residents on two fronts: (1) The traffic on Ives Dairy Road was already clogged; rezoning would result in total gridlock, and (2) Our lush green 8ackyard (the golf course) was to 8e replaced with a view of town homes and seven story condominiums. The 8itter dispute ended with Williams Island o8taining rezoning permission from the commissioners. Williams Island sold the golf course to a real estate developer for a reputed $23 million dollars. At this writing, four years later, the once lush green golf course is an unattended 158 acre weed pasture, home to insects and rodents.

NOTES

Sales Promotions

It may come as a surprise to many of my dear readers that there is more to running a jewelry store sale than just hanging up a few sale signs. Preparing promotional sales is a profession of itself. Effective advertising must be individually tailored to fit the store's personality, which is beyond the capabilities of local newspapers. In many sales, -- not all – merchandise tie-ins with the ads must be supplied; sometimes the window and in-store displays must be completely re-arranged. A well planned storewide sale requires additional sales clerks, which included my service. I am not a super salesperson, but what I brought to the sales were proven, effective merchandising aids. Although every store's advertising program was different, one thing they all had in common was an increase in the sale of their diamond and gemstone jewelry, the mainstay of a jewelry store's business. This synopsis is not meant to disparage the ability of many jewelers who conduct do-it-yourself sales. I simply filled a niche to jewelers, mostly in small towns, who lacked the background and/or the inclination to attempt the undertaking on their own.

NOTES

Catalog/Showrooms

Their origins can 8e traced to the marketing distri8ution chain that was in place at that time for many consumer products: manufacturer > wholesale distri8utor > retail store > consumer. To name a few of many of these products (some of which have disappeared): Westclox and 7eth Thomas clocks, Community and 1847 Rogers Bros. silverware, Corning Ware, Ronson lighters, 7haeffer and Parker pens, GE small appliances, Panasonic Electronics. On most of these items, the retail stores made a 40% profit on the selling price and the wholesale distri8utor made a 25% profit of the selling price to retail stores. Thus when a wholesale distri8utor of those products opened its door and sold directly to the pu8lic at the same price as it sold to retail stores, the consumer saved 40%.

NOTES

Jerome Grossman

Jerome, who was a great friend and mentor, passed away at age b4 in 2003. He had left Helzberg's and joined H & R Block, America's largest income tax preparers. Officially he became the vice president in charge of Mergers and Acquisitions, but unofficially he was one of Henry's closest advisers. (Henry is the "H" of H & R Block; Richard, the "R", had been stricken with cancer and retired from the business). I have been told by many knowledgeable Kansas City businessmen that Jerome played a leading role in H & R Block's phenomenal growth.

GLOSSARY

A Brachah (Blessing)

The point of this joke is an attempt to illustrate how far the Jewish religion has evolved from the Eastern European immigrants, who were all Orthodox Jews (the Christian equivalent of born-again evangelicals) to the Reformed Jews who, in the opinion of all Orthodox Jews, had abandoned the Jewish religion. Hence, in the joke when the Reform rabbi was asked, "What's a brachah?" he personified the Jew who doesn't understand a word of Jewish.

INDEX
Of family, relatives, friends and associates.
Names as they appear in the 8ook
Followed 8y page num8er(s).